HOW NOT TO RUN FOR PRESIDENT

Catherine Clark

SCHOLASTIC INC.

To my daughter, who's full of new ideas

ISBN 978-0-545-49848-7

Copyright © 2012 by Catherine Clark.
All rights reserved. Published by Scholastic Inc.,
557 Broadway, New York, NY 10012, by arrangement
with Egmont USA. SCHOLASTIC and associated logos are
trademarks and/or registered trademarks of Scholastic Inc.

12 11 10 9 8 7 6 5 4 3 2 1   12 13 14 15 16 17/0

Printed in the U.S.A.   40

First Scholastic printing, September 2012

ACKNOWLEDGMENTS

I had the good fortune to have an editor who closely follows politics and has a good sense of humor, so a huge thank-you to Ruth Katcher. When I came up with this idea, I had no way of knowing it would end up being your project. How lucky for me!

Thanks also go to Erin Downing and Jill Grinberg, for writerly support; Amy Baum, for telling me about upper registers; Laura Morlock, for lending me her clarinet; and of course, Ted and Cady. Cady, you will be taking clarinet lessons soon, so just accept it.

Standing there in my uniform, I felt like I was about to faint.

I couldn't tell if it was the hot, humid July day making me dizzy or the fact I was nervous about playing my clarinet in front of so many people.

Or was it the tall, poufy, fake-fur marching-band hat that was making even my ears sweat? Up until then I didn't know ears could sweat. Stupid band hat.

My best friend, Simon, did a few drumrolls. "Can we start already?" he asked. He adjusted the neck strap that held his snare drum in place. If he tripped, it would strangle him.

"Um, I think that would miss the point," I said. "The big shot's not even here yet."

I'd never seen so many reporters and video cameras. TV news crews from Cleveland, Columbus, and who knows where else were on the square to cover Governor Bettina Brandon's presidential campaign stop in our small Ohio town.

Tons of citizens were sitting in folding chairs, perched on curbs, or milling around downtown— hundreds of people, probably thousands, at least half our town and many more from neighboring ones. Everyone wanted to meet Governor Bettina Brandon on her latest tour through Ohio. Everyone wanted to hear what she would say. Maybe today was the day she'd announce her pick for vice president; maybe it would even be someone *from* Ohio. She was the independent, Internet-sensation candidate for president, the governor from Minnesota who'd created the Fresh Idea Party, otherwise known as FIP.

When I got the call from my band teacher Sunday night, asking me to come to an emergency rehearsal, my mom had been excited; she likes Governor Brandon because she's a woman and a mom and because she's in a third party, which means she was "outside the political machine."

What machine? I didn't see any machine. What would it do, anyway? Produce senators and presidents the way our town's FreezeStar factory produces refrigerators, ovens, washers, and freezers?

My mom told me that Governor Brandon was running against two guys who were insiders and didn't care about small-town people like us. One was a Republican senator named Fred Flynn, and the other was a former Democratic vice president, Jack Mathias.

Mom had bad things to say about each of them, but I didn't really know much about them or about the election. Dad was voting for Senator Flynn. He'd already made up his mind, he said.

It was a very close race, and from what Mom said, getting closer all the time.

The three candidates were virtually tied in the latest polls, which was supposedly unheard of for a third-party candidate, never mind a woman. My mother was very excited about Governor Brandon. Mom said she stood for people like us in towns like ours, or something like that.

All I knew was that neither of the other candidates had come to see us, so maybe my mom was right.

I looked around the crowd. The Fairstone Fire Department was out in full force, along with the sheriff, state troopers, and us, the Fairstone Ferrets middle-school marching band. We'd been roped in to play with the high-school band to give it bigger numbers—and we'd only practiced together once, the day before, because the campaign had just announced two days ago that they'd be coming here.

It definitely had the makings of a bad performance, but thankfully, we were only playing patriotic numbers, songs we all knew well.

"Well, if I stand here in this uniform any longer, I'm going to pass out." Simon peered at the sun as if it were an evil being, robbing him of his power.

If he were a superhero, his weakness wouldn't be Kryptonite—it would be ultraviolet rays. Simon has sandy-brown hair and lots of freckles—he can sunburn in five minutes flat.

I hate the middle-school band uniforms. They don't match the high school's new ones at all. In fact, they're so old, they're historic. We look like an army from a country that was killed off in a war.

Our uniforms consist of blue jackets with brass buttons and shoulder pads. White ropes and tassels hang off the shoulders. The pants have white stripes down the outer sides. Oh, and everything smells like mothballs. And we have to wear spats.

Spats are white, plastic, fake-leather things that you put over your required black shoes or sneakers so everyone appears to be wearing the same shoes.

Girls' shoes.

At least, that's what they look like.

So there we stood, waiting, and feeling slightly ridiculous, right in the midst of news vans, satellite trucks, fire trucks, sheriffs, and state troopers. Up on the grandstand, which was made of bleachers brought on trucks from the football field, I spotted Mayor Lewis, his wife, and their annoying son, T.J., who had just finished sixth grade with me.

T.J. officially stands for Tyler James, but in my head I always think of him as "That Jerk."

Even though he was way up there on the grandstand,

I could guess what T.J. was thinking. I could read his very limited mind, which was thinking, *Don't tell me you're playing. I'm going to pummel you after this, Shrieking. I'm going to take your clarinet and bash you in the Shrieking gut.*

He said that to me whenever he saw me with my clarinet, which was how I knew it must be in his thoughts. He's boring and unoriginal that way. My last name is Schroeckenbauer, which is too hard for him to say, so he just calls me "Shrieking."

But then I looked closer at T.J. and saw he was playing with one of those wooden paddles that you bounce a red rubber ball against. That would take up all his brainpower for at least ten minutes. As my dad would say, he isn't the sharpest knife in the drawer.

"I really hope T.J.'s dad doesn't introduce him to the governor," I said to Simon. "Can you imagine how much he'd brag about that? We'd never hear the end of it."

T.J. tends to act very important just because his dad is the mayor. Also, he is really good at sports and about half a foot taller than me and Simon.

"I hope she doesn't end up hating our town. Probably take away all our funding," Simon said.

"We get funding?" I asked.

Simon rattled the drums. "Did you pay *no* attention in current events?"

5

"I paid attention plenty," I said. "Go ahead. Ask me who the sixteenth president was."

Simon did a quick drumroll, then said, "Abraham Lincoln. And that's way too easy—everyone knows that."

Ms. Stoneburg, our band teacher, was making her way down the line, handing out bottles of cold water. I glanced at my watch. The governor was supposed to have arrived an hour and a half ago. She wouldn't be a punctual president, that was for sure. That probably mattered when you were meeting people like other presidents and prime ministers. She would have to work on that. All I knew was, this definitely wasn't the way *I* would run for president.

I glanced around the crowd again, looking for my family, and spotted T.J. making his way across the town square. He was headed for the food carts. Big surprise.

I recognized him because of his buzz cut and the fact he has this wrinkle on the back of his neck. It isn't fat, I swear. It's muscle. Everything about him is muscle.

Cotton candy was just one of the weird things in the middle of town that day—we usually only have that at the county fair. There were hot-dog, popcorn, and ice-cream carts cluttering the sidewalks.

But that was a good thing. Eating cotton candy would keep T.J. occupied long enough so that he didn't think up some new way to torture me or mock me in my band uniform.

T.J. lives to threaten me. I've gotten used to it over the years, and a lot of the time he doesn't do anything about it, but that doesn't mean I like it. Since we live in a small town, we see each other all over the place, whether I want to or not. It isn't like we have four sixth grades. We only have one.

But I was not going to let T.J. ruin the day for me. This was a major event, covered by national news media. And I had a clarinet to play.

Behind me, a couple of seventh-grade girls were warming up on their flutes. They sounded completely out of tune, but it was hard to tell who was the worst.

As my clarinet teacher, Mort, always tells me, "Flute players are a dime a dozen."

Two eighth graders were competing to see whose trumpet could blare the loudest. Meanwhile, our best saxophone player was away at basketball camp, and her backup sounded out of tune. The high-school band was trying to keep its distance from us, even though we were all supposed to be playing together. Ms. Stoneburg kept pacing back and forth, looking nervous, which wasn't very reassuring. Was she thinking, like I was, that this performance was going to be a major disaster?

Suddenly, I spotted a motorcade pulling up on

Main Street. Two motorcycles rode ahead of a big tour bus. As it passed us, I saw BRANDON: THINK FRESH and VOTE FOR THE FRESH IDEA PARTY! in huge, bright green letters on its side.

Behind it were more vehicles: SUVs, a limo, and several white news vans with satellite thingies on top. They parked on the grass, and soon men and women in suits were fanning out around the bus. I noticed that most of them were wearing wires in their ears.

"She rates Secret Service agents? Cool," Simon said.

"I don't know why they call them secret," I said, watching them move through the crowd. "There's nothing secret about them." If you wear a black suit in our town and there isn't a funeral or a wedding, you pretty much are going to stand out.

"Let's try to meet them," said Simon.

"I don't know. They might shoot us," I said.

"Good point," Simon said. "But let's get a little closer so we can get a better view."

"But we're playing soon—"

"We'll have plenty of time to get back." Simon pushed forward, using his drum to gently nudge people out of our way.

Just then, I saw a couple of the agents parting the way for the governor as she stepped down from the bus. She was followed by a girl around our age, who was followed by even more agents and other people. It was like a clown car.

We got close to the grandstand, which was decorated with red, white, and blue streamers and balloons. There were giant BRANDON: THINK FRESH and BRANDON FOR PRESIDENT signs everywhere: on the podium, tacked to trees and light posts. Two women in a Fresh Idea Party booth were selling bumper stickers, buttons, and T-shirts. On the grandstand, a banner was whipping like a flag in the hot wind.

The grandstand was in front of the town hall, where the governor was going to speak. Our downtown is historic. Sometimes I think it looks like an old Western movie set, like if you pushed gently on any of the fronts of the buildings, they'd fall down. Some of the stores are vacant.

Those "hard times" everyone on the news keeps talking about? That economic crisis or whatever? It was born here. It lives here.

A reporter paused in front of me and Simon. "Zoom in on that 'Going Out of Business' sign right there, over their heads," he told the cameraman. "Then back to me." He cleared his throat and spoke into the camera. "Doesn't this signify the effect the recession has had on our country? Look at this town. Once a thriving center of industry, now hanging on by a thread. And so the new economy bites another victim. Score: New Economy: one, Fairstone, Ohio: zero."

"Did he just call us a zero?" I asked Simon.

"I want to clock him with my drumsticks," Simon said.

Suddenly, the reporter seemed to notice us. "How about you guys? Would you care to comment on the election?" He pointed his microphone toward us.

I stared at the black, spongy microphone, stalling for time. It kind of looked like a Whac-A-Mole hammer—or maybe that was just my mood. "Um, no thanks," I muttered.

Simon shook his head.

"But surely you have something to say," the reporter pressed. "You're in one of the most hotly contested battleground states in the country. How exciting is it to have Bettina Brandon in your town today?"

"We just found out, uh, Sunday, so I haven't had that much time to think about it," I replied. "But it's cool. Really cool."

"Is it the coolest thing that's ever happened around here?" the reporter asked us.

"What? No way!" Simon practically pushed the reporter to grab a chance at the mike. "Last year the girl's basketball team went to state. *That's* the most exciting thing that's ever happened here," he said.

"Let me rephrase the question," the reporter

said. "What are the most important issues facing the country today?"

Issues facing the country? Was I really someone who could comment on that?

I adjusted my giant puffy band hat. A clump of fake fur was missing on the side because our dog, Sassafras, had gotten hold of it one night, thinking it was a cat, I guess, and fought it to the death.

And then suddenly, there was Governor Brandon, standing right behind the reporter, looking tall and imposing. She had short blond hair, and she was wearing a sleeveless dress.

"Yes, I'm interested to hear what you think," Governor Brandon said with a smile. "Fresh ideas come from young people. So, what's the biggest issue facing your town?"

The reporter and cameraman pushed in even closer, zooming in on the two of us, framing the shot. I bit my lip and looked around the town square, stalling for time.

Behind the governor was the blond girl I'd seen getting off the bus with her. I figured she was her daughter, because she was wearing a name tag that said EMMA BRANDON. She was dressed in a sleeveless dress like her mother, only she had a pink sweater draped over her shoulders. Like she would need one when it was eighty-five degrees. In the shade.

"Well, uh. How about the, um, new healthy plan—health plan? If we were healthy, we wouldn't need a plan, would we? So why don't they call it a sick plan?" I asked. "Anyway," I said, coughing, while they all stared at me.

I started thinking about my asthma, which can flare up when I get nervous or when there are dozens of idling cars, buses, and news vans nearby spewing exhaust in my face. Like right then.

I must have been taking too long to think about it, because the reporter cleared his throat. He glanced at the candidate and then back at me. "What's your name?" he asked.

"Aidan," I croaked. "Aidan Schroeckenbauer."

The reporter nodded. "I'll get you to spell that for me later. Okay, Aidan, this is your big chance. If you had one question to ask a future president, what would it be?" he asked.

I looked behind him, up at the crowded bleachers, at everyone in town, sitting and waiting and hoping for some good news. I spotted my parents: my dad, who'd normally be sleeping now because he works third shift and doesn't get home until eight in the morning. My mom, who'd been laid off a few months back and was getting really tired of not working. I thought of how they argued, day after day, whenever they saw political ads on TV.

My dad was rooting for Senator Flynn for

12

president because he promised he'd keep jobs in the United States. My mom said that was unrealistic and that we needed a balanced approach like the one Governor Brandon proposed. She also said that Dad, Senator Flynn, and former vice president Mathias did not know what they were talking about and were complete, out-of-touch idiots. (She tends to get easily upset these days.)

Governor Brandon leaned a little more closely to me. "Don't be nervous. You can ask me anything— I'm all ears. Other candidates talk and talk. Their mouths are open, but their ears are closed. Me, I listen."

"Okay. Then, uh, what will you do to keep manufacturing strong and save jobs?" I finally asked. "Because FreezeStar is the biggest employer here, and my mom already got laid off in the last big round of cutbacks, and my dad's salary has been frozen for two years, which is kind of funny because, you know, the company is *named* FreezeStar."

The governor just looked at me. She did not laugh. "Not a lot of people are buying new appliances right now, I guess," she said, looking concerned. "This recession has hit us all hard."

"Right. If the company doesn't make it, we have no Little League sponsor. Also, the funding for band and music class has been cut, so FreezeStar has been donating money to support that. And if the company folds, my mom says we'll lose our health insurance, and then I won't get my asthma meds, and I'll completely fall apart. Basically, what I'm saying is that one company can really make a big difference, and, like, our whole town will shut down if FreezeStar closes—"

As I was rambling, I saw a large metal campaign sign blowing in the hot summer wind, swirling from side to side. Two corners came loose—then suddenly it broke off the podium above us. It was plummeting right down at Governor Brandon's head! I had to save her!

I handed my clarinet to the reporter, leaped toward the governor, and shoved her out of the way.

"Uh—sorry! I'm so sorr—" I started to say to Governor Brandon, who was lying on the town square beside me. Fortunately, we'd smashed onto the grass, not the historic brick.

"It's all right—I'm fine," she said. "Nice save!"

I started to get up, but two guys in dark blue suits immediately flattened me to the ground.

I couldn't breathe. One of them had his knee on my chest. The other one held a gun, pointed at my neck. "Don't shoot!" I yelled.

"Why shouldn't I?" the taller one asked in a deep, intimidating voice. "Give me one good reason. You attacked—"

"I didn't mean to! I was trying to protect her from—" I said in a desperate, pleading tone. Couldn't they see I was just a kid? Did they really think that I was making an assassination attempt?

"Explain yourself!" the shorter guy yelled in my face.

I stammered, "The—that sign—it was falling—"

"Who made it fall? Who made it fall?" he kept demanding, shaking my shoulders.

"N-no one! Nothing!" I said. "I mean, maybe the wind?" I actually had no idea, but I had to say something.

The tall one peered into my eyes, and I felt like a criminal being interrogated under a big, bright lightbulb. "What are your intentions?" he demanded.

"That big sign was falling, and I didn't want it to hurt her, or anybody else!" I tried to get up, and they flattened me to the ground again. This was getting old.

They suddenly lifted me in the air as if I were a doll, one carrying my arms, one carrying my feet. They hauled me over to a police car and stood me up against it. Then, just like on a TV crime show, they frisked me. They checked under my arms. They emptied my pockets. They examined everything and then dropped it to the ground in a heap: coins; my house key; my bike-lock keys; a folded-up, half-eaten box of Lime Brains; my inhaler.

"Kid. You need a purse or something," the tall one said when he was done checking me for weapons.

"I'm a *boy*!" I said. Of all the indignities.

"Oh, right. Right. Sorry. Couldn't tell with that uniform." He peered at the shiny white spats on my feet, covering my sneakers. "Nice spats. You're a boy. For real?"

"Yes," I said through the dirt and grit in my teeth. That was it. I was never wearing that uniform again. Also, maybe Mom was right. Maybe I did need a haircut.

"Well. I don't see anything that makes me suspicious, so I can guess we can let you go." The shorter one brushed off his hands. "But watch your step from now on. And do us a favor: don't try to do our jobs."

"I wasn't—I mean, sure, right. Sorry," I said. I didn't tell them that I wouldn't have had to do what I did if they had been *doing* their jobs and paying better attention to the governor.

"Here, I think this is yours." The reporter handed me my clarinet.

"Thanks," I said, nodding. I was glad I hadn't been holding it when they frisked me. They probably would have broken it in half to make sure it wasn't a weapon.

I leaned over to pick up the rest of my stuff from the ground and jammed everything back into my pockets, then put my ridiculous band hat back on my head. Maybe I could blend in with the rest of the marching band. I rubbed my wrists, which were sore from being held behind my back. If I never got frisked again in my entire life, that would be too soon.

"I knew we should have screened these kids," the shorter Secret Service agent was saying.

"These kids? How about this entire town?" the tall agent replied, brushing off his suit sleeves.

"What's wrong with our town?" I asked. "Why does everyone keep bashing Fairstone?"

"Sorry, no offense. We just—these events really strain our resources," he said. "She wants to go everywhere, talk to everybody, twenty-four/seven. She has to go to every coffee shop, barbershop, bowling alley, grocery store. It's difficult to keep up." He turned away from me and started talking into a headset mouthpiece.

While Governor Brandon visited with the Fairstone firefighters who were hanging her sign back up, her daughter just stood there, smirking at me.

"Kind of short to be in a marching band, aren't you?" she said. "That hat is taller than you."

I glared at her. She was taller than me, but so what? So were a lot of girls in my class. That didn't give her the right to insult me about it.

She glared right back, like a mirror image of instant hatred. "Fine," she said. "Notice you didn't try to save *my* life."

"I don't even know who you are," I said, which wasn't true. But I didn't want her to think any more of herself than she apparently already did.

"Obviously, I'm Emma Brandon," she said, pointing to her name tag. "Or can't you read?"

"I can read just fine, thanks," I said. "I don't know about you."

She stuck out her tongue at me. Really? I thought. Was that the best she could do? How old was she, anyway? She dressed like she was a grown-up, but she acted like she was five.

"Well, Emma, are you making friends?" Governor Brandon asked as she turned back to us. She straightened her skirt and patted her hair into place.

Not exactly, I thought. Making enemies, maybe.

Emma just shrugged, knocking her sweater off her shoulders and onto the dusty sidewalk. "Rats!" she complained, picking it up. "I hate this thing."

"Emma, dear. Don't say 'rats,' and don't say 'hate.' Language matters, remember?" her mother asked.

"Rats," Emma muttered. "I wish it didn't."

"Well, it does." The governor looked like she was blushing as she turned to me. "Thanks to you, I don't have a concussion. Emma, are you all right?" she added.

"Mom. I was standing here the whole time," Emma whined, rolling her eyes. "I'm fine."

She's all right, except for being snooty and stuck-up, I wanted to say.

"Okay, Governor, time to keep moving. We need to get up to the grandstand now!" A well-dressed woman in a business suit gently tried to pull her away.

Instead of leaving, the governor smiled at me. "You sure *you're* okay?" she asked.

I nodded. Except for being completely embarrassed, I was fine. She was being so nice to me. I didn't know what to say. "My mom is a huge fan of yours," I blurted out.

"Oh, thank you. Please tell her thank you for me. I'd like to meet her. Is she here?" she asked.

"She's somewhere up there, but I don't see her right now," I said.

"Maybe later, then. So, as you were saying, it's very important to keep manufacturing jobs here in the U.S." She continued talking to me, but more to all the reporters and other people who were suddenly gathered around, about unions, manufacturing, cars, factories, and how towns like Fairstone were the jewels of the Midwest. Of the United States, actually.

A guy with square black glasses and spiked hair tapped her gently on the elbow. "Governor, we really need to get moving and start your speech—"

"I know, just give me a second here, Stu. What was your name again?" Governor Brandon asked me.

"Aidan." I skipped my last name this time around.

"Aidan. Nice name. I have a nephew named Aidan. He's crazy about LEGOs, but he's a lot younger than you." She smiled. "You know what, Aidan? I don't even know if everyone here knows this, but *I* used to play the clarinet."

Behind her, I saw her daughter roll her eyes again, as if she'd heard this story a hundred times.

"Really?" I squeaked.

"Yes, really," she said, nodding. "I played all through high school and was even in marching band, like you. What do you think? Maybe you could play a little something for me?"

My mind went blank. What could I possibly play in a situation like this? Was there a song about knocking down a presidential candidate?

"Well, actually, our whole marching band is about to play. . . ." I looked around, feeling helpless. Where had everyone gone? Why was I the only one left standing there?

Then I realized they had all lined up outside the hardware store the way we were supposed to, getting ready to play. They'd deserted me. Even Simon was gone.

I stalled for time, adjusting the clarinet reed in my mouth. I considered taking off, running for the hills, as they say. But then I thought, no, I was good at playing clarinet. Why had I been taking lessons for the last few years if not for a moment like this? This was easy.

"Everyone, make room!" Governor Brandon said. "Back up. Give him some air. Ladies and gentlemen, I give you Aidan!"

I had a vague sense of video cameras being aimed in my direction, and the sun reflected off one metal microphone, nearly blinding me for a second. I took a deep breath, closed my eyes, and launched into "America the Beautiful."

Unfortunately, I was so nervous that the top notes came out bleating, like wounded sheep.

I hoped my clarinet teacher, Mort, wasn't listening. This would break his heart.

When I finished, there was scattered, awkward applause from the governor and her helpers, like when someone at the Super Bowl screws up the national anthem by forgetting the lyrics. Except worse.

The governor gave me a sympathetic pat on the back, then jogged off toward the grandstand to make her speech. Following her was that annoying Emma, smiling as if I'd just made her day. The clump of reporters went jogging after her, and I was left alone. For a second.

Then I noticed T.J. standing a few feet away. "Way to go, Shrieking!" he said, gloating. "Way to make our town look bad."

"What? I didn't make the town look bad," I said.

"Maybe not, but you made yourself look terrible."

He guffawed. "You tried to kill the president, Shrieking."

"I didn't—and she's not—"

"You were almost arrested. Ha!" He laughed. "That would have been so cool, seeing you dragged off to jail. My dad would have locked you up."

I simmered. He didn't know anything. The mayor doesn't do the locking up. The warden does, or, in our small town, probably the sheriff. T.J. didn't even understand the legal system. If anyone would be headed to jail in the future, I was guessing it would be him.

"At least I can play an instrument," I said. "At least I can read music—"

"You know what?" he said. "Your playing? Your tackling her? It's going to be all over YouTube."

I tried to pretend this wouldn't bother me. "So what?" I asked.

"So, I'm going to enjoy it. Every single minute of it," he said, grinning.

This was about to go on record as one of the worst days of my life.

I heard the marching band start playing by the hardware store, and I hustled over to take my position. Maybe no one would notice me from now on—if I were lucky.

3

"I've seen better swings on a porch, Aidan!"

A lot of insults get hurled in Little League batting practice. You get used to them. Maybe that one doesn't sound so bad, but it was coming from my *uncle*.

Because Uncle Robert is a high-school gym teacher, he has the summers off, so he was coaching our summer league at FreezeStar Field. It was a step up from having T.J.'s dad as coach. He'd quit because he was too busy being mayor, or so he said. I never saw him do much but stand around and try to look important.

Anyway, it was a nice change, even if Uncle Robert could be insulting at times. It worked out perfectly, because my younger cousin, Liam, would be old enough to play at this level next year. I've always wished my dad could coach, but he can't, because he works the night shift. He shows up for practice when he can, like this evening. I always want to do really well when he's around.

I hit some nice grounders off the next couple of pitches, but then a pitch went wild and I had to duck before the ball bonked my helmet.

"Thanks a lot!" I yelled to Colin, our third-best pitcher.

"Lime brain!" he shouted back at me.

Sometimes I can't tell if the point of baseball is winning or just surviving.

T.J. was up next, so I handed him the bat, but he tossed it on the ground by the dugout. I should have remembered. He always uses his very own special bat, the one he won't let anyone else touch.

"You don't usually get a crowd for a practice. What gives?" my dad asked as I joined him in the home dugout.

"We've got a celebrity coming. Governor Brandon's on her way." Uncle Robert kept throwing a baseball into his glove, over and over. "Her staff called me, said she wants to drop by and see the company-sponsored team."

While they talked, T.J. was booming hits over Colin's head, deep into the outfield.

"So that's why all the news vans are parked over there?" my dad asked. "For a photo op? Typical woman," he added. "Wanting all the attention."

"What?" asked Uncle Robert. "Why would you say that? She's running for office. She needs to be in the news every day, for good reason."

"Well, Flynn doesn't do that," Dad muttered.

"Be serious. Everyone in the race does that!" Uncle Robert cried. "Besides, Flynn's never met a camera he didn't like."

"And neither have you," Dad said to Uncle Robert, who was combing his hair.

"Ha-ha," Uncle Robert said. "Who'll be laughing when you look horrible on TV and I don't?"

"That's what I'm trying to tell you. The whole election, it used to mean something. Now it's all photo ops. Zero substance," my dad argued. "Same goes for this Brandon."

"I don't know, I think she's really got something with her Fresh Idea Party. And at this point, I don't care if it's a woman, a man, or an alien with three heads," said Uncle Robert. "Just as long as she gets something *done* if she gets elected. She's for the little man, right?"

"I guess so," said my dad.

"Well, then, that'll work for you," my uncle teased him.

Simon and a few of the other kids burst out laughing. My dad glared at Uncle Robert. "And if she knows how to represent stupid people, *you're* in luck."

Everyone laughed again. My dad and my uncle could trade insults all night, and they often did.

My dad is short, and so am I, but it's nothing

off-the-charts short. It's just that Uncle Robert is a grizzly bear in comparison.

They mostly get along, but every once in a while their friendly teasing seems like it could erupt into a fistfight. I wouldn't want to see my dad lose.

And he would. Badly.

It's kind of like me fighting my big brother. I wouldn't attempt that. Christopher has about a foot of height on me, and too many pounds to think about. Plus, he knows how to fight. I don't.

I sat there for a minute and watched T.J. crush the ball over the heads of the guys playing outfield. He was an amazing hitter. You can't take that away from him.

Actually, I can't take anything away from him. He's too strong.

I play shortstop. I love my position, except for the fact it has the word *short* in it. Why does it have to be called that? There's first baseman, second baseman . . . Why not stopman? There's catcher, pitcher . . . Why not stopper? It doesn't help that when my grandma comes to games, she yells, "Way to go, shortie!"

Like a lot of shortstops in history, I'm a better defensive player than a hitter. Not that I put myself in their league, but the same was true of famous shortstops like Ozzie Smith, Omar Vizquel, and Ozzie Guillen.

Sometimes I think I should change my name to

start with an *O*, to give myself better odds of making it to the big leagues. Oidan. That sounds weird. Forget it.

Then again, that would leave out Derek Jeter, and I wouldn't want to do that. I love the Yankees. I know it's wrong because I live in northwestern Ohio, and I should love the Cleveland Indians. I do, I totally do, and going to an Indians game last year with Simon was awesome, but I also just love the history of the Yankees.

Dream #1: Go to a Yankees game at Yankee Stadium. Dream #2: Go to the Baseball Hall of Fame in Cooperstown, New York.

Neither of those places is even *that* far away. But it had been taking a long time to convince my parents we should go.

The Football Hall of Fame? Oh, sure. We'd already been there, because Christopher wanted to go. Not only was it in Ohio, but what my brother wanted, he usually got.

I know my dad tries to treat us equally. He just can't help it that he's more interested in Christopher's athletic career than in mine. Or that he doesn't come to all my band concerts because they tend to be at night, when he works. He's never really gotten why I like the clarinet. Football is a lot easier to understand, and I can't really blame him for that.

Sometimes it feels like our family has two sides:

me and Mom, and Christopher and Dad.

We heard cheers coming from up on the embankment. I saw the Fresh Idea Party bus pulling up to park on the side of the road, where minivans usually took up the spots.

"Here they come!" said my dad. Everyone in the field came over toward the dugout to get a better view. Uncle Robert flipped a little mirror out of his pocket, whipped off his baseball cap, and started to fix his hair.

"Again?" my dad groaned. "What, you think you're going to be on TV or something? Do you really think they want to get a shot of you?"

"Shouldn't you be leaving for work?" Uncle Robert replied, waving his comb in the air. "Besides, you only wish you had something to comb."

All the guys on the team, including me, were staring at the bus, the news vans, and the Secret Service agents who were stepping out onto the grass. Our grass. Our ball field.

Secret Service agents fanned out around the bus and started to cross the field. Then the governor came down the steps, flanked by more agents, and headed toward us, followed by about a dozen other people, including her daughter.

The governor was trailed by a few campaign workers, who were reading their BlackBerries or texting into iPhones and Droids while they walked.

Reporters were walking after them, holding out microphones and looking desperate for a good story. One woman's high heels kept sinking into the soft field, and she almost fell down.

Governor Brandon was smarter. She had changed into jeans, a Cleveland Indians jersey, tennis shoes, and a baseball cap that said BRANDON FOR PRESIDENT.

Trotting beside her was her daughter, wearing shorts, a T-shirt, and a Minnesota Twins ball cap. Her ponytail stuck through the little hole in the back. She was smiling and looked like a normal girl. That was strange.

Maybe she had one of those split personalities, like those psycho villains in movies. One minute they're normal, the next completely merciless.

"Look out, everyone. Look out!" the taller Secret Service agent said. "Coming through." He stopped and looked at me. "You again?"

"Hi." I gave a pathetic little wave.

He narrowed his eyes at me, then kept going.

Governor Brandon seemed surprised to see me standing there. "Hey! Aidan, right? I know you." She grinned.

"Hi," I said.

"Yeah, you should remember him. He tried to *kill* you," said T.J.

I glared at him. "Be quiet."

Emma stood beside her mom, chomping on a

piece of gum. She looked around at the FreezeStar Field. "Well, this field needs some work, doesn't it?" she commented.

"It's Little League," I said. "And it's pretty nice. What do you expect, Yankee Stadium?"

"No. It's just . . . the grass is turning brown. My Little League field is way nicer," Emma said.

"Emma. That's not polite," her mother said. "I'm sorry. I think she's homesick. Mind if we play along for a little bit?"

"Oh, sure, sounds great," said Uncle Robert, looking nervously from mother to daughter and back again.

"Excuse me, sir." A tall African American man who was also wearing a BRANDON FOR PRESIDENT ball cap, along with a matching campaign button on his white button-down shirt, held an Indians ball cap out to Emma. "Here you go, Emma," he said. "Wear this."

She looked at it as if were poison. "What? No way! Why would I wear that?"

"Because the campaign manager wants you to," the man said. He tipped his cap to us. "Nice to meet you all. I'm Governor Brandon's campaign manager. Retired General Roy McGarvin."

"Nice to meet you, General." Uncle Robert shook his hand. "I recognized you right away. You were secretary of defense under the last administration."

"That's right." The general nodded. "And secretary of transportation before that. And now, Emma, back to you. Enough already, just wear the home-team ball cap. Is that too much to ask?"

"It's not fair," she said. "The only thing I know about the dumb team is that they stole our best player, Reed Jackson."

"Cleveland didn't steal him—he was a free agent," I said.

"Same thing," she said, hands on her hips. "And what about Hayashi? He was our best relief pitcher. You stole him, too."

I looked at Simon and shrugged. What could we say? She was right about that. I was a huge fan of Hayashi and his split-finger fastball.

"Wear it, Emma," the general said in a stern but friendly tone, "or you don't play."

"Fine." Emma took off her Twins cap, handed it to him, and jammed the Cleveland one over her head.

"Sometimes being in charge of an entire platoon was easier," General McGarvin muttered to Uncle Robert before he headed off, pulling out his cell phone.

"I'll take first base," Emma announced. "That's what I play at home."

T.J. was already on his way to first base. He stopped and stared at her. He looked like he was going to burst. "But that's my position—you can't—" he spluttered.

"Can't what?" She straightened her ponytail and jogged out to take his place at first. He started running beside her, but she won. "You're out," she said as he touched the base after her.

T.J. stood in the infield, looking lost, as if he wasn't sure what to do. Then he walked over to me and said, "Fine. I'll play shortstop, then." He pushed me out of position.

Emma looked at me and cracked her gum. "Well, I'm going to need a glove."

"Emma," her mother said. "We talked about that."

"My glove?" Emma asked. "I know. I told you I shouldn't have left it at home!"

"Not that. Gum!" her mother said. "You're not to crack your gum in public like that."

"Fine," Emma said. She dug a small hole in the ground with her heel, spit her gum into it, and covered it up with dirt.

Her mother frowned. "That wasn't exactly what I had in mind."

Because of the way Emma did that, and since she had stood up to T.J., I kind of liked her a little more than I had earlier. Besides, he'd already pushed me out of my position. What was I going to do, push out someone else? I'd never do that.

"Here, you may as well take mine," I said, holding out my well-worn glove.

She looked at it as if it were a dead fish, her lip kind of curled up to one side. "Okay, thanks, I guess," she said. Then she slid it over her left hand and punched the heel a few times. "Let's play ball!"

I was happily on my way back to the dugout to watch when Uncle Robert stepped out from behind the plate, sliding up his catcher's mask. "Since you just gave up your glove, Aidan, why don't you hit?" he asked.

What? "Me? Why me?" I said.

"That'll be great. Mind if I pitch?" asked Governor Brandon.

"Uh, well, no, I guess—that'd be fine," Uncle Robert stammered. He handed the baseball to Governor Brandon.

"It's okay—I won't break it," she joked as she strolled out to the mound. "I played a little softball in college."

"*Mom.* She was All-American," Emma said loudly. "Why do you tell them the boring stuff and skip the cool parts?"

"That was a long time ago," said the governor. "But I think I can still get the ball across the plate."

Colin frowned at her, then jogged past me, toward the dugout.

"You want to hit?" I asked him.

He glared at me. "What do you think?" Colin tossed his glove on the ground and sat down on the bench to watch.

I knew what he was thinking: why did they think they could just show up and take over our practice? At least, that's what I was thinking.

I grabbed a bat and stood at the plate. I took a couple of practice swings while Governor Brandon warmed up her arm, lightly tossing the ball back and forth with Uncle Robert and the kids in the infield, including Emma. Our dugout had been temporarily taken over by campaign workers like the general. I glanced over at the photographers and reporters standing by the third-base line. There were even a couple of video cameras filming the governor. Over on first base, Emma was punching my glove and bouncing on her toes.

Uncle Robert tossed the ball back to the governor one final time, then crouched behind me. "Okay, Aidan. Hit one for the hometown. Make me proud."

I set my stance and waited for the governor to wind up.

Governor Brandon's first pitch blew past me like a freight train.

Uncle Robert cursed as the ball hit his glove.

"Aidan! Look alive!" my dad called from the dugout.

"My grandmother could have hit that ball!" Emma shouted from first base.

Governor Brandon threw a few more pitches before I had a chance to even get my bat on the ball. When I did, I knocked it foul, over my shoulder.

I started thinking that maybe she should quit politics and go into professional softball.

"Rotate!" Uncle Robert called, and T.J. jogged straight for home plate.

"I'll go," he said. "So we can show them that someone in this town can actually hit a baseball."

"Ha-ha. Very funny," I said. I was more than happy to trade places with him.

T.J. handed off his glove to me like a football, slamming it into my ribs.

When we quit practicing about fifteen minutes later and I walked over to the water jug, T.J. was showing Emma the video he'd taken earlier in the day with his smartphone. In it, I was tackling the governor, then getting hauled away by the Secret Service and frisked. T.J. had zoomed in and captured the grass in my hair and the dirt in my teeth. He, Emma, and the rest of the team were laughing hysterically as they watched it. Even Simon, that temporary traitor.

"This is classic!" Emma took an iPhone out of her pocket. "I totally have to add that to my favorites."

"Totally," I muttered.

T.J. started telling Emma how many views it already had on YouTube.

"Don't you have anything better to do?" I asked him.

"Not really. This is pretty sweet." He hit PLAY again, and he and Emma laughed as they watched the Secret Service agents pulling endless stuff out of my pockets and mistaking me for a girl.

Fortunately, Governor Brandon came over just then. "What are you guys laughing at?" she asked. "Not my pitching, I hope?"

"Oh, no, Mom. It's nothing," Emma said, shoving her phone into her pocket. She must have had practice at covering for herself.

"If you say so." Governor Brandon turned to T.J. "And who are you? I'm afraid Emma took your spot at first base."

"I'm T.J.," he said. "T.J. Lewis?"

Short for That Jerk, I wanted to say.

"My dad's the mayor?" T.J. added.

"Right, right! Fantastic! Hey, how about a picture?" The governor posed with him while reporters snapped a couple of photos. That Jerk was getting good press while I was being made to look like an absolute fool. When was he going to end up on the losing side of things, for once?

The general came over to say something to the governor. She looked at her watch. "Well, it's been a pleasure, everyone, but we have to get going. Thanks again, Aidan," she said to me.

"For what?" I asked.

"Everything. Saving me from that plunging sign, a concussion, or worse! And you really got to the heart of what this election is all about. Keeping jobs close to home and keeping small towns strong." She nodded. "From now on, I'll always think of Fairstone when I talk about those issues."

Ha! So there, I wanted to say to both T.J. and Emma.

"Oh. I almost forgot." Emma held out my glove. "Thanks for letting me use this, but you really need a new one. This thing is falling apart."

I glared at her. She couldn't even say thank you without insulting me. "No problem," I said coldly.

I watched the entire group tromp across the field, up the embankment, and back to their Fresh Idea Party bus. If that was the last time I ever saw them, I was definitely okay with that.

When I came down for breakfast Wednesday morning, my brother, Christopher, was having a fit. "Mom, seriously. Seriously. How do you expect me to keep up and not be totally embarrassed—"

"If you find a job this summer, we can talk about getting cable again." My mother tapped a few commands into her cell phone and smiled at me as I sat down at the kitchen table. "Oh, good, you're finally up!"

"You know, Mom. You don't *need* a cell phone," Christopher argued. "If you got rid of yours, then we'd have enough money for cable—"

"Zip it, Christopher," my mom said. "I do need a phone. I have to keep up on Facebook." She looked over at me and smiled again. I noticed she had dark circles under her eyes, as if she hadn't slept well. She tended to get insomnia a lot these days.

"Humph." My big brother was watching ESPN's *Baseball Tonight* on the tiny TV that's mounted under the kitchen counter while he ate a big bowl of chocolate frosted flakes. "I can't believe they're doing this to us. Can you believe it?" he asked me, slouching like nobody's business. "Not only do we give up this"—he pointed to the TV—"but Internet, too? I mean, way to kill any fun around here, Mom."

I think it was about the fifth time he'd watched the same *Baseball Tonight* program. He was making a point, not that it was having any effect on our parents. It was our last day of expanded basic cable, and we were all in mourning. Just another one of the sacrifices Mom and Dad kept talking about, because of the so-called new economy.

Of course, I know other people have it much worse. Even Simon, who ended up moving when his parents couldn't make the payments on their house. Now they live in this apartment complex across town and it takes us twenty minutes to ride our bikes to see each other. Plus, he has to share a room with his brother Henry. Who's two.

Anyway, for me one thing that really stinks about your parents getting laid off is giving up things like cable. Especially when you're a baseball and football fanatic like Christopher, or just a regular baseball fan, like me.

"You have your phone," Mom said calmly to Christopher. "Just be thankful for that for the moment."

"I could use a phone," I said.

"Yes, you have a point," she agreed. "We'll talk to your dad about that."

"Seriously?" I squeaked.

"Wait a second. Why is *he* getting something?" Christopher complained. "You keep saying how we have no money."

Good question. There was something strange about Mom's supremely good mood. She was dressed nicely, too, as if she might have a job interview. "Mom? Are you going back to work or something?" I asked.

"Nope," she said cheerfully.

"You should. Then we wouldn't have to give up cable," said Christopher.

"Don't you think I would go back to work if I could?" my mom asked. "Honestly, Christopher. You don't grasp what's going on here. You need some of Governor Brandon's common sense."

While I was wondering what that meant, Mom turned up the volume on the TV. The anchor was saying, "Folks, there are rare moments when the sports world connects with the political scene. Last night was one of those nights." The video clips showed the two other presidential candidates throwing out first pitches: Flynn at a minor-league game somewhere in the South, and former vice president Mathias at a Yankees–Red Sox matchup.

I couldn't help noticing that they didn't pitch

41

nearly as well as Governor Brandon. Flynn's pitch went wild and nearly beaned a bystander, while Mathias didn't throw the ball hard enough to even reach the catcher at home plate.

The anchor continued, "On a separate note, let's check in with Governor Brandon, who threw out the first pitch at a Little League game in Ohio last night—"

"What first pitch? It wasn't even a game," I said. "It was practice!"

"Nice arm," Christopher commented as he watched the clip. "She's got heat on that thing."

"Tell me about it," I grumbled. "I couldn't hit a one."

"Not much else went right for the Fairstone Freezers," the reporter said.

"Freezers?" Christopher exclaimed. "Can't they even get the name right?"

"These kids may not be headed to nationals, but they've got as much guts as any other team out there." Then they showed me playing shortstop, grabbing a ball, and rocketing it to Emma at first. "The shortstop's name is Aidan Shriekingbaum. Throwing to first, where the governor's daughter also showed some serious skills."

"Schroeckenbauer," Mom said. "It's not that hard to say!"

"You may be hearing more about him in the future," said the reporter. "This is the same kid who saved the governor from falling scenery earlier in the day." While he spoke, the replay of my heroic deed played on a large screen behind him. They had it in replay mode, so it repeated over and over, then backward. "He's fast on his feet, America."

Christopher looked at me with newfound respect. At least I think it was respect. I didn't get that look much, so I wasn't sure I'd recognize it if I did. "You're just an average kid," he said, sounding jealous. "Why do *you* get featured?"

I shrugged. "I must have done something right."

"Your fielding is good, but only because of what *I've* taught you," said Christopher.

"Right," I said. "It has nothing to do with the fact that I've studied the game on my own or practiced or anything."

"Exactly," Christopher agreed, pushing his chair back from the table. He refilled his bowl of cereal while Mom changed the channel to a local morning show.

"Check this out," she said. "You're all over TV." She switched from channel to channel. "I've been dying for you to get up so I could show you! You know the phrase 'overnight celebrity'? That's you, Aidan."

On every station, the news of the hour started with a clip of me: Me pushing Governor Brandon to safety. Me talking about saving jobs. Me playing "America the Beautiful" on the clarinet and squeaking on the high notes. Everyone kept calling Ohio a "battleground state," whatever that meant. Did people really fight during presidential elections? The last time it had happened, I'd been only eight, and I hadn't noticed. I thought they just went into voting booths and pressed buttons.

Each reporter had a different, corny way of putting it.

"What started as a minor scuffle and a mistaken identity has turned this young boy—"

"I wish they'd quit calling me a *young* boy," I said. "I hate that. I'm not young."

"Nice band uniform," Christopher said, laughing. "They *carried* you? I totally missed that. Oh, that's awesome."

Stupid girly spats on my feet. Stupid band hat that looked like a sheep on my head.

"What one young Ohio boy did today could change the course of the election," said a reporter on another channel.

"Or not," Christopher said, laughing. "Could your hair look any worse? Helmet hair, dude."

I slumped down in my seat, wishing I could be invisible. Maybe it was a good thing we were losing cable. Maybe *everyone* should give up cable.

In the past twelve hours, according to my mom, my face had been on CNN, Fox News, MSNBC, NBC, ABC, and CBS. It was on Web sites, social media, everywhere. My mom had been up since five watching TV. She said she couldn't sleep well, so she'd decided to get up and enjoy our last day of cable.

Mom wasn't quite herself these days. One day, a few months ago, she'd gotten laid off, just like that. No advance warning. She and my dad argued a lot about money now, but never directly in front of us. It was awkward, to say the least.

Lately, she'd been shuffling around in her robe, doing crosswords and watching too much TV during the day, so then she couldn't sleep at night. She kept downloading recipes she'd never cook and redecorating ideas she would never try. She had printed pages of this stuff, scattered on the coffee table. Then she and my dad would argue about where she should keep it all. He'd put it in a notebook, and she'd take it out and say he had put the pages in the wrong order.

Just then, Dad's pickup pulled up in the driveway as he got home from the overnight shift. He goes to work at midnight and gets home after eight.

A minute later, he ducked through the front door, while our dog, Sassafras, barked and growled. When I looked outside, I saw that our lawn and driveway were full of reporters, shouting questions.

"That was insane," said my dad. "Do you know how many people are out there? We're in the spotlight, for sure."

"It's all because of doofus here," said Christopher. "He's like the MVP of YouTube."

"Hey, one of them said I was good on defense!" I spoke up.

"They tried to interview me at work, but the security guards wouldn't let them in," said Dad.

"Why not? What are you hiding?" I asked.

"Nothing!" Dad said. "It just cuts into our work to have visitors."

"They're worried about spies picking up on trade secrets," said my mother.

"Yeah, right!" Christopher laughed.

Neither my mom nor my dad joined in.

"Seriously?" I asked. "Spies at FreezeStar?"

Dad nodded. "Not that there are any now, but corporate espionage is something we all need to be prepared for," he said. He sounded like he was reading from an employee handbook. "In the new economy, there may be threats we haven't anticipated."

If I heard anything about the "new economy" one more time, I was going to hit someone. Every time we heard it, we got one more thing crossed off our Christmas or birthday lists.

All of a sudden, Sassafras started barking again like crazy.

"Someone's at the door," Mom said.

Christopher and I ran over to the living-room

window and looked outside, parting the curtains. A taxi had parked behind Dad's pickup, and three people emerged. They all looked familiar from the day before.

One was the tall, bald, African American general who had insisted Emma wear a Cleveland Indians baseball cap. He was wearing khakis and a crisp, white button-down shirt. The other man was much younger, with square black glasses and spiky hair. He had his tie flipped over his shoulder and was texting into a phone as he walked, plus he was having a conversation into an orange headset. The third person was a woman with short, dark hair who'd been hovering beside Emma the day before. She was wearing a business suit and walked briskly up to our front door.

"Great, more reporters," Mom said as she prepared to open the door.

"Actually, I think they're—" I started to say.

"Get rid of them," Dad said.

"Get rid of them?" Mom asked. "Why would I do that?" She opened the door and smiled. "Hello. May I help you?"

The general smiled politely. "Good morning, ma'am. Is Aidan home, ma'am? We'd like to talk with him, if we could."

"That depends. Who are you?" asked Mom.

"We're with Governor Brandon's campaign," said the younger man, stepping up. "My name is Stu

Brautigham. I'm the assistant campaign manager. Can we talk?"

"Full-time assistant campaign manager," the general said, "and part-time haircut."

"And this is General Roy McGarvin, US Army, Retired. Everyone calls him the general," said Stu. "We run the campaign together. And this is Kristen Lindgren, part of the governor's personal detail."

The woman held out her hand to Mom. "I'm also a very loyal campaign worker, and a governess for Emma," Kristen said. "It's a pleasure to meet you."

"Wow, this is amazing," Mom said. "Anyone who works for the governor is a friend of mine. I absolutely adore Governor Brandon. She's got my vote. Come on in!" She shook their hands and stepped back to let them into the house.

Kristen, Stu, and the general walked into the house. Kristen waved at me. "Hello, Aidan."

"Hi," I said, still wondering what they were doing at our house.

"What's a governess?" Christopher asked. "Is that like an actress?"

"Not exactly. It's like being a governor, only I'm in charge of one person instead of a state." Kristen smiled. Christopher still looked confused, and I felt the same way. "I keep track of the governor's daughter," she explained quickly. "Make sure she stays out of trouble."

"It's not an easy job," General McGarvin said with a frown.

"Listen, Aidan," Stu said. "We're here because if we've heard one thing in the last twenty-four hours, it's this: everyone is really impressed by you. People admire what you said, and what you did."

I laughed. "What did I do, exactly?" Besides embarrass myself on national television?

"Yeah, really. Which part? When he couldn't hit a pitch, or when he butchered 'America the Beautiful'?" Christopher asked.

I looked at him. I didn't need that kind of help.

"Listen, let me tell you. We managed to spin that whole thing. Actually, other people did it for us," Stu said. "Now all anyone can remember is that you saved the governor from a potentially life-threatening head injury and that you care about the election. So they even have a name for you."

"Who does?" Mom asked.

"This should be good," Christopher said quietly.

"The press! Haven't you heard? They're calling you the 'clarinet hero.'" Stu grinned. "Pretty cool, right?"

I smiled. I kind of liked the sound of that. I didn't think I'd ever been called a hero before.

"Ridiculous." Retired General McGarvin rolled his eyes. "Everyone overuses the word *hero* nowadays. Used to *mean* something."

"Oh." I looked down at my shoes.

Stu coughed. "What the general is trying to say is that this was Governor Brandon's YouTube moment, the one that pushes her over the top. You were there, kid. You made it happen."

The general cleared his throat. "In fact, we're here because we'd very much like you to come on the campaign trail with us. With Governor Brandon."

What? "Will I get a horse?" I joked. "You said trail, so . . ." Nobody laughed. I was starting to think they weren't the joking kind.

The general narrowed his eyes at me. "You don't know much about politics, do you?"

"Not really." I shrugged. I've taken social studies like any other kid, but that's about it. "I did a project on John Glenn once," I added. "Famous, uh, astronaut, senator, Ohioan."

"We *know* who he is," said the general.

"Perfect. You're so perfect." Stu looked at me and smiled.

"Oh. He's a dream come true for this campaign," said Kristen. "No question. We may need to cut his hair, but . . ."

"Oh no, I say keep the hair," said Stu. "Authentic kidness."

"If that's what you think, then we'll definitely have it cut," said the general. "ASAP."

Why was everyone suddenly talking about me

as if I weren't in the room? I coughed loudly, in case they'd forgotten I was still there. "You know, maybe you want my brother, Christopher, to go instead of me," I said. "He's older, and he's very, uh, photogenic."

Christopher smiled his school-picture smile, the one that makes tons of girls want to go out with him. Personally, I think it's a little cheesy.

The general studied Christopher for about a half second. He seemed to be scanning him for known viruses. "No. I don't think so. No, thanks."

Christopher frowned. He wasn't used to getting rejected, and I felt sorry for him all of a sudden. I could give him about a dozen pointers on rejection. He's been sheltered all his life, because he's good at everything and doesn't know what to do when he isn't. "But he's older," I argued, "which means he can vote soon."

The general laughed. "This isn't about who can vote! It's about the future of our country. It's about appealing to a broad base. You do that." He ran his hand over his bald head, as if he still had hair there. "Don't know why, but you do that."

I raised my eyebrow. "That's the deal? Really?"

"Really." He nodded.

"Really?" I asked again.

"Kid, I don't have time for this," said the general. "We're leaving town in an hour, as soon as the governor finishes the pancake breakfast at a firehouse a couple of towns over. Pack a suitcase and get ready."

I gulped. *Me? On the road with them? Seriously?*

In a weird way, I liked all this attention. I felt like a superstar. But in another way, I did not want any attention paid to me at all. I wasn't comfortable with the spotlight. So far it hadn't been very flattering.

"He's too young to travel around like that, isn't he?" said my dad.

"No, he's not," said Mom.

See? They can fight about anything. If Mom says the sky is blue, Dad says it's red.

"Well, I say he is," my dad insisted. "We don't even know you people, and you want him to go away with you? Why should we let you?" He tended to be a bit overprotective of us.

"Because it's for Governor Brandon's campaign," my mom said. "I'd do anything for her."

"You don't know *her*," my dad pointed out. "You know her image. That's not necessarily the same thing."

"With Governor Brandon, it is," the general argued.

"He'll have a chaperone," Kristen said. "Me." She smiled. "I'll make sure you dress appropriately, act appropriately . . . and don't do anything to raise questions about the candidate. Mr. and Mrs. Shrabeckenstauer—"

"Shroeckenbauer," my dad said. "It's not that difficult, is it?"

"My apologies, Mr. Schrookenbear," said Kristen. "Aidan will be in good, good hands with us. I'll watch him like a hawk. I won't let him out of my sight."

"Well, to take care of any worries, what if you let me come with Aidan?" Mom asked. "I'm a huge, huge fan of the governor's, and I'm not working right now, so I'm able to travel. I could volunteer, pitching in doing whatever needs to be done for—"

"I'm sorry, ma'am," the general interrupted. "That's impossible. We haven't had time to properly vet you."

"Vet me?" Mom asked.

"We'd have to do a thorough investigation before we added an adult to the campaign. Aidan's a kid, so he has no history," said the general.

Since when did I not have a history? I'd written my autobiography in fifth grade for school. Maybe it was only two pages, but I did have a history.

Besides, this was my mostly mild-mannered, PTA-joining, brownie-baking, Christmas-pageant-planning mom. What could she have ever done that would get her into trouble?

"If you're worried about being lonely, Emma will be on the bus with you, remember?" Kristen smiled. "You two can be friends. She is a lot of fun."

I remembered the gum-cracking, glove-stealing girl from yesterday. Fun? *Really?*

"We also have lots of perks," Kristen explained. "The bus is totally high-tech, with Internet, satellite TV, video games, catered meals, a fridge full of soda and snacks—"

"Who cares about the perks?" my mother cried. "This is about an election to save our country. This is your chance to make a difference, Aidan."

Stu snapped his fingers. "Exactly. You gave the campaign a much-needed bump. Your job is to get Governor Brandon the small-town vote, the youth vote, their parents' votes."

"Why can't Emma help you with all that?" I asked. "She's a kid." Even if she was aggravating in almost every way.

Stu shifted in the chair and adjusted his tie. "This is different. People have read about you. They know you. You're a valuable commodity to the campaign. You're an outsider; she's an insider."

Funny, but I thought it probably had more to do with the fact that she was completely annoying. "I just . . . I don't know," I said. I walked to the wide sliding door in the dining room and looked out at the deck and our backyard.

Summer was for hanging out, for doing nothing except playing baseball, riding my bike, swimming at the reservoir. Why would I want to be shipped off with this group? It sounded like joining the army—especially with General What's-His-Name in charge. I was way too young for that.

Dad came over to stand beside me. When he spoke, he kept his voice low. "What are you thinking?" he asked.

"I kind of want to go. But then . . . I don't know," I said.

"I'm the same," said Dad. "It's an amazing opportunity. I'm proud of the way you spoke up. But, you know, they're talking about stealing you for a couple days."

"Dad, they're not stealing me," I said.

"Yeah, I know. But when you're a dad, you'll understand." He fiddled with the vertical blinds on the door, trying to get them all to face the same direction. "Like it or not, you're a celebrity now. You can't just disappear. You may as well try to get some issues out there, if someone's willing to listen to you."

I thought about what the governor had said to me the day before, how the other candidates talked too much and never really listened. "But who's going to listen to me?"

"I don't know, but I guess some people are, Mr. Clarinet Hero. Look, this is a chance of a lifetime. You might be able to change some things, or at least put us on the map. You'd be helping the town."

Only if I don't mess up, I thought.

"Think of how much it would mean to your mom," he said.

The fact he wanted to make my mom happy—I couldn't resist that. His eyes had dark circles under them, and I realized that no matter how tough things had been lately, he'd hardly ever complained. What if I could do something to help everyday workers like him? The company, or the town?

"We'll miss you," he continued. "But I bet it'll only be a week. Knowing this crew and the way candidates change their minds, maybe only a couple of days. You won't miss summer—don't worry."

"But you don't even want to vote for her," I said.

"Not yet," he agreed. "Maybe she'll say something to make me change my mind. Maybe you'll help her sort out the issues. Maybe you'll be the one who convinces me to vote for her."

"So . . . you think it'll be okay?" I asked. "For real?"

"Definitely." He nodded. "It's a gut feeling I'm getting, just so you know. I usually rely on those. I think these are good people. I think you'll be safe with them."

"Okay, then. I'll do it," I said. We both turned around, ready to go tell the group our decision.

Before I could say a word, the general said, "Listen, kid. We're getting nowhere here, and we're out of time. What's something you really, really want?" The general sighed, as if he was running out of steam.

I could tell him I was already planning to say yes, or I could hold out for something good. I had to think for a minute. I had a long list, but there was one thing I'd been dying to do for years. "I've always wanted to go to a Yankees game. At Yankee Stadium," I said.

"Done. We'll get tickets for your whole family, we'll fly you to New York—"

"And my friend Simon," I put in. "He needs to come, too."

"And your friend Simon," the general said. "Fine. Done and done. But hurry and pack. We've got to strike while the iron is hot. Everyone, meet us outside FreezeStar in an hour."

"What—what do I bring?" I asked, but they were already gone, out the door, off to their waiting taxi.

Mom, Dad, Christopher, Sassafras, and I stood in the doorway, watching them go.

Before he got into the cab, Stu turned back toward us. "Oh, and Aidan?" he yelled. "There's just one thing Governor Brandon wants you to promise you'll bring with you."

"What's that?" I asked.

"Your clarinet!" he called. Then he slipped into the taxi and closed the door, and the car flew backward out of the driveway.

What had I gotten myself into?

5

"Now, you'll call us, right? So we know you're okay?" my mom asked me as we got out of the car at the giant gray FreezeStar plant. Either we were a little early to meet the bus or the bus was late, as it had been the day before. Either way, it was fine with me. I wasn't sure I was ready to leave yet.

Whenever I stand anywhere near the FreezeStar plant, I feel like a tiny bug. It's so huge that it takes up at least fifteen acres. There was a large, random group of people gathered outside the huge main parking lot to see me off.

Word had gotten around quickly, and I blamed it on Christopher. He and his friends were always texting, arranging last-minute parties, and he'd been at it for the last hour, while I was packing.

"How am I supposed to call you? I don't have a phone," I said.

"You'll borrow one from that Stu guy. Did you see him? He has about twelve going at a time," my dad said.

"I still can't believe they want you and not me," said Christopher, shaking his head.

"What's that supposed to mean?" I asked.

Instead of answering, he disappeared into the crowd to find his friends. I couldn't believe he'd take off at a time like this. No, not because I was leaving. It was that he was missing the chance to be photographed repeatedly. Knowing him, he'd be back as soon as the reporters arrived with the Fresh Idea Party bus.

"Well, then, call us as soon as you get a chance," my mom said. "Check in at least three or four times a day."

"Do we want him spending his time seeing the world or calling us?" asked my dad.

"I'm not going to see the world," I said. "The rest of Ohio. Pennsylvania maybe."

"Oh, I don't know about that. I bet they keep you all the way to the Beltway," said my mom. She kept brushing tiny specks of lint off my red Ohio State T-shirt and smoothing my hair back. It felt like Christmas family-portrait time.

"The Belt-what?" I said.

"Washington, D.C.," she explained.

"I don't know about this." My dad frowned. "I still think this candidate is all photo ops, zero substance."

"Dad," I groaned. "You said that yesterday."

"No, she's not," my mom said. "She has lots of substance. She has more nuts and bolts in her campaign platform than either of the other two guys. She makes good, honest common sense."

"Maybe so, but she's not ready," my dad scoffed.

"And I think *you* aren't ready for a woman president," said my mom.

"What?" Dad looked at her as if she were crazy. "That's not it at all."

"Then what *is* it?" Mom asked.

"*She's* not ready," said Dad.

"What are you talking about? She has just as much experience as the other guys, if not more!" said my mom. "She's been Minnesota's governor for four years. She's run a household, she's a lawyer, she's served in the state senate, on the PTA—"

"The PTA?" My dad started laughing. "Since when does that qualify you to be president of the most powerful country in the world?"

"Have you ever *been* to a PTA meeting?" my mom shot back. "You know, it's just like FreezeStar," Mom said. "Guys always support other guys. The guy managers make more than the women managers. The pay scale isn't even. The—"

"Sh!" my dad said. "You can't stand here outside FreezeStar and criticize the company. What are you, crazy?"

My mom poked him in the chest. "If anyone's crazy around here, it's—"

Before she could finish her sentence, I walked off to see if I could find Simon to say good-bye and ran smack into Mort, my clarinet teacher. I'd called to tell him I wouldn't be able to make my next few lessons. His assisted living place wasn't far from the FreezeStar plant, so he'd walked over. Even at eighty-nine, he was pretty spry.

Mort was always complaining how the FreezeStar trucks rolled all night and beeped when they were backing up. "The other oldies in here can't hear worth a lick, so it doesn't bother them," he'd always say. "But me, I can't sleep. Ears are too trained."

Most people probably haven't heard of Mortimer Wrute, because most people don't keep track of clarinet players in history, but until he retired, he played with famous orchestras in London, Berlin, and New York. Then he played with the Cleveland Philharmonic Orchestra for the last twenty years of his career. He was a real master.

That's my plan—or one of my plans, anyway. Play the clarinet, see the world. I know the odds are against me. How many brilliant clarinetists does the world need, anyway? But maybe one day I'll be as good as Mort and become one of them.

"Aidan, tell me again why you're going on this tour," Mort said now. He was sipping a coffee he'd picked up from the McDonald's across the street. He went to McDonald's every day for a free coffee, which he called the only benefit of being eighty-nine years old. "Why are you heading out of Fairstone with a bunch of unknowns?"

"Because they asked me," I said.

"And would you jump off a short pier into a dry lake if they asked you?" Mort said. "I mean, really. You can say no."

"But . . . I don't want to say no. I never get to go anywhere," I said. "Look at you. You've traveled all over the world. I haven't been anywhere except Cleveland and Columbus." Besides, I kind of liked the attention. But I didn't want to admit that to anyone.

"Yes, but you're only eleven," said Mort.

"Twelve," I said.

"Right, twelve." He looked at me for a second. He held a hand over my head, then compared it against his height. "You're short for twelve."

Why did everyone have to point that out? "I was a preemie, remember?" I took up wind instruments when I was six because my doctor, who's Mort's son, thought it would help me improve my lung function. I was born a couple of months premature, and because of that, or because of some other unknown, unfair reason, I have asthma.

Back then, I could hardly hold the clarinet right,

because it was nearly as big as I was. At least that's how it felt. So Mort actually had me start with the recorder and then move up after a couple of years, when my hands were big enough. I've been taking clarinet lessons from him ever since, and I'm getting kind of good. He thinks I have "the gift," anyway.

Since my asthma is under control, I can play Little League and basically do anything I wanted. Sometimes when I have a cold or run too much in cold weather, I can have an asthma attack, which was why I have to carry my inhaler with me all the time.

"Ah, I was only kidding you," said Mort. "Don't take everything so seriously." He sipped his coffee.

There was something I had to ask him, and I was dreading it. "Were you, uh, there yesterday?" I asked. "When the marching band played? Or actually, before they played, when I, sort of, uh, played?"

"I was. And, quite frankly, there are some things it's better not to talk about," Mort said.

My heart sank. I hated disappointing Mort. He worked so hard to get me into performing shape. And there I'd been, mangling an historic, patriotic anthem.

"It's like I always tell you, Aidan. Make every performance better than the last." He coughed. "Which shouldn't be too hard. On the plus side, people are talking about restoring the music program cuts. So maybe your performance wasn't pointless after all."

I didn't know whether to be glad or humiliated that my clarinet performance was inspiring my school to bring back music education.

Mort pointed to the clarinet case in my hands. "Glad to see you're planning to keep practicing on the trip."

"Yeah, for sure," I said. "Actually, to tell you the truth, it was Governor Brandon's idea."

"What—why? After yesterday?" Mort looked perplexed. "It wasn't your best day, kid. That's all I'm saying. I know you're a lot better than that. But does she?"

"She told me she used to play clarinet. Maybe she wants to play duets or something," I said.

Mort groaned. "Too gimmicky. Doesn't she know that? Clinton tried it with the saxophone back in ninety-two."

I'd had to memorize the presidents, in order, for a history test last year. William Jefferson Clinton. Number forty-two. "President Clinton won," I said, after a moment.

Mort frowned. "Yes, but that's not the point."

"What is the point?" I asked.

"She's not going to win by playing the clarinet on a late-night talk show!" Mort cried. "If that were true, any Tom, Dick, or Harry would be president."

I didn't recognize the names. "Who?"

"It's an expression," Mort explained. "I'm saying that she needs to back up her philosophy with concrete proposals." He shook his head. "And would it kill her to announce her pick for vice president? If she doesn't get her act together, she's not going to have a chance."

"I thought she had a third of the votes in the latest polls," I said.

"Those numbers are fudged," Mort said. "They move them around like cards in a three-card monte game, keep people confused until they pick the wrong candidate. Before you know it, the game's over and you've lost."

Wow. I had no idea he was so bitter about politics and politicians. If that were true, why wasn't he *for* Governor Brandon and her fresh ideas? I didn't know what to say. "Well, I probably won't be gone long. And she promised to get me and my family tickets to a game at Yankee Stadium, so . . . I'm going to go."

"Make the best of it, then," Mort said. "Use the platform."

"What platform?" Why did everyone keep talking about a platform? Did this involve diving?

"You know, you're up there on the national stage now. Use the opportunity, the fact that people are listening to you," said Mort. "Talk about how music funding for schools is being cut. How there's nothing left. How this country will never again produce a generation of musically literate citizens."

I stood there, wondering how I was going to remember all that and say it as well as he did.

"And," said Mort, "practice every chance you get. And don't let her make you play anything juvenile and embarrassing just to suit her."

"I won't," I said.

"'Happy Birthday.' 'Itsy-Bitsy Spider.' Forget about it," said Mort. "Flat out refuse. You have standards."

I nodded. "Sure. Definitely."

"And don't forget what pitch means next time!" he called over the sound of the approaching Fresh Idea Party bus as it pulled in and came to a stop.

First the team of Secret Service agents got off and scanned the area, communicating over their ear wires. Shortly after that, the governor got off the bus to shake hands and talk to people heading in and out of the parking lot. I couldn't help noticing that Emma didn't even get off the bus. She was probably too snobby to do parking-lot events.

"Hello again, everyone," Stu said, coming up to us. "We'll be leaving in a couple minutes. You ready, Aidan?"

I nodded. "I'm ready. I guess."

Mom and Dad each gave me a giant bear hug. Mom also gave me about a hundred different pieces of advice to pass on to Governor Brandon. Dad just told me to have fun and order room service and bill it to the campaign. "Maybe then she'll understand how taxes and fees add up," he said.

"What's that, Mr. Schroeckenbauer?" asked Governor Brandon, suddenly standing at his elbow.

"Oh, uh." Dad got all flustered. "Nothing."

"Believe me, no one wants to raise taxes in this financial climate," the governor said. "I hear you."

Mom just stood there, looking starstruck to be in the governor's presence. She didn't speak.

"I'm so glad to finally meet you both." The governor held out her hand. "Bettina Brandon. Thanks for lending us your son for a few days. We'll take good care of him—I promise." She leaned closer to Mom. "And, as one mom to another, you know I'll watch him like a hawk."

Mom laughed. "Make sure he keeps his hotel room neat. And if he says he's brushed his teeth, check his toothbrush. And—"

"Mom. I think that's enough," I said under my breath, but suddenly it was like the two of them were best friends. Mom couldn't stop talking.

Then Kristen was giving my parents all the contact information they'd need, plus a link to "follow the bus" online.

Finally, Simon pushed his way through the crowd to us. He was panting and out of breath. "Sorry I'm late. I had to ride my bike to the store to get you something first."

"You didn't have to get me anything," I said.

"Sure, I did. You won't survive without these. Here." He gave me a giant box of Lime Brains candy.

"Thanks," I said. "I will need these. I think I'm going to be bored out of my skull," I whispered to him.

"Yeah, but at least you're getting out of town," said Simon.

"Good point." I decided to wait and tell him about the trip to Yankee Stadium later, when I got home and it was more of a sure thing. "I wish you could come," I said.

"Yeah. That'd be cool. Make sure you get all the perks. Order room service, charge up video games, junk like that."

"Aidan, it's time to go!" Stu called from the bus steps.

"Well, see you," Simon said. "Have fun being famous!"

Just before I walked away, T.J. made his way around the reporters and pushed up right beside Simon.

"You really should thank me, Shrieking," he said. "Without that video I took, nobody would even know your name."

"You're not the only one who made a video,"

Simon said. "What, you think you're the reason he was picked? Be serious."

"Yeah, well, I'm glad he's leaving," T.J. said. "Because with him gone, we can actually win a baseball game!" T.J. laughed loudly.

All the reporters standing around the bus started laughing. Maybe getting out of town for a while wasn't such a bad idea, I thought. "I'll really miss you, T.J.," I said. "Not." I picked up my clarinet case, a backpack with my baseball glove and a baseball inside, and my duffel bag full of clothes and other assorted junk, and climbed onto the bus.

I passed by the general, who was jotting down notes about a mile a minute on a legal pad. He glanced up at me. "More kids on the campaign trail. As if one wasn't enough? Now I've seen everything."

"I thought this was your idea," I said.

"Nope. This came from the Haircut," he said, going back to his notes.

"The Haircut?" I checked out his bald head. He clearly wasn't referring to himself. Then I remembered that was his nickname for Stu. I wondered if he had a nickname for me. Maybe, Needs a Haircut?

He looked up again and focused on me. "You know the old saying? If you're the president and you want a friend in Washington, get a dog."

"Yeah—uh, sure," I lied.

"A dog," he repeated. "Not a kid from Ohio."

Great, just great. The general hated me.

I smiled at him, hoping he wouldn't kill me, and looked down the aisle for an empty seat. Suddenly, I spotted one with my name on it—seriously, there was a sign that said AIDAN S. taped to the headrest. It was right behind Kristen, the governess, who was knitting.

"Don't let the general get to you," Kristen said. "Deep down he's a nice guy."

"How far down do you have to go?" I asked.

She laughed. "Oh, I was a little worried about you, but I think you'll do just fine." She waved her knitting needles in the air, and I saw that she was knitting a sweater with an American flag pattern. "By the way, I have a fifth-degree black belt in karate. I'm an expert at self-defense. And, I could pierce someone's heart with one of these needles from thirty feet away," she said.

"Uh, okay," I said, noticing how strong her arm muscles looked.

Kristen smiled. "Just kidding about that last part. All I'm trying to say is that you're safe with me, okay, Aidan? No worries."

"Right. Sure," I said. "No worries." As long as I stayed on her good side, that is.

She smiled. "Have a seat, why don't you? We're about to hit the road."

Across the aisle, Emma was sitting with her feet up, acting like I didn't exist. She had a small computer on her lap and didn't look away from it.

"Emma. Is that how we greet someone?" Kristen asked.

Emma smiled like it was killing her. "It's a pleasure," she said in a monotone. She cracked her gum.

"Emma! Please don't do that," said Kristen. "How many times do I have to tell you?"

Emma rolled her eyes at me and shifted slightly in her seat, snapping her laptop closed. "Where did you get that bag? Don't you have a real suitcase?"

I glanced at my blue duffel as I wedged it into the rack above my seat, along with my backpack. On the side, it said, FREEZESTAR: KEEPING IT COLD FOR 75 YEARS. "What's wrong with it?"

"Nothing. It's just not a real suitcase—that's all," she said.

I sat down and placed my clarinet case on the aisle seat beside me. Oh, boy. She was going to be such a fun travel companion. "It's called a duffel bag. You wouldn't know because you're not an athlete."

She raised an eyebrow and cracked her gum again. "I saw you play yesterday. You're not much of an athlete, either."

I glared at her. I'd thought she was sort of cool when she'd played baseball with us, and she had

71

even stood up to T.J. But that might have been the only good thing about her.

The bus was pulling onto the turnpike, approaching the tollbooth.

When I was younger I thought it was actually called a trollbooth, where a troll waited to attack when you tried to collect a ticket. My brother made sure I never forgot that. "Here it is, pipsqueak, the trollbooth!" he always yelled, and I'd cower down in my car seat.

I was trying not to be a wimp, but I couldn't help feeling a little scared. Not because of the trolls but because I didn't really know where I was going. I didn't know the people I was going there with, either. I felt excited but also kind of sick to my stomach.

This trip wasn't going to last long, I told myself, remembering what Dad had said. Plus, I was doing this for Mom. If I could make a difference, I would. But . . . how?

"So. Is that a clarinet, or what?" Emma pushed at my clarinet case with her foot.

We'd been on the turnpike for half an hour already. She'd scooted over from her window seat across the aisle, while her mom was up front in the couch area, having a strategy meeting with Stu, the general, and assorted other campaign workers. I'd never seen so many BlackBerries, Droids, and iPhones all being used at once. It was like a cell-phone orchestra. From what I could tell, everyone was scouting the next stop, checking the polls, making plans for future appearances.

"Yes. It's a clarinet," I said. Didn't she know that? Hadn't she been there when I embarrassed myself with "America the Beautiful"?

"You know, I didn't get a chance to tell you yet, but I'm a musician as well," Emma said. "I'm a flutician."

"What's a flutician?" I asked.

"Obviously, a flute player. First chair," she said.

"Uh, you sound like someone who gives people their shots and stuff. A flu-tician," I said.

"And you sound like someone who is not educated about music," Emma said. "At all."

If she wanted to get into a music feud with me, she would lose. "Well, it's called a flautist," I corrected her.

"I know. I know that," she said. "I was testing you, obviously."

"Obviously," I repeated. "Yeah, right. I'm sure."

There wasn't much to like about her, but then, who else was I going to talk to? I couldn't sit there and talk politics for hours. I couldn't even talk politics for five minutes.

"So, do you always travel with your mom?" I asked. "I mean, where do you live when you don't live on the bus?"

She didn't say anything for a second. She just stared at me, as if I were the dumbest ape on the planet. "Don't you know?"

"No," I said. "If I knew, why would I ask?"

She rolled her eyes. "You can't be serious."

"I'm not serious," I said. "I'm Aidan."

"Ha-ha. So funny," she said. "I can't believe you don't know."

I shrugged. "Well, I don't. Do you know where I'm from?"

"Obviously. We just stopped there. Freestone," she said.

"Ha! Wrong," I said. "Fairstone."

"Same difference," she said.

"It is not!" I said.

"Excuse me, but you're a nobody. My mom's the governor of Minnesota, so obviously, I live in Minnesota." She pronounced "sota" like "soda."

"So, you live in Minneapolis?" I asked.

She sighed, as if that was the dumbest thing she'd heard all day. "Saint Paul," she said. "That's the capital. Which is where the governor lives. *Obviously.* In the governor's mansion."

"Whatever," I said. Was she going to use the word *obviously* in every sentence? "So what's Saint Paul famous for?" I asked.

"Lots of things." She sniffed. "Tons of things."

I waited for her to give an example. "It's so famous you can't think of anything?" I asked.

"I can, too!" she said. "The Mississippi River."

"That's more of a claim to fame for Mississippi, isn't it? Or else it'd be called the Saint Paul River," I said.

She frowned at me. "It starts in Minnesota. Everybody knows that. It comes from Lake Itasca."

"Oh. Well, we have Lake Erie," I said.

"We have Lake Superior," she replied. "It's the biggest of the Great Lakes."

"I know that," I said. Humph. Did she have to have the greatest of the Great Lakes? "Okay, so you have lots of water. Anything else? Besides freezing-cold weather?"

"There's tons more. Winter Carnival, awesome skiing and snowmobiling, the state fair every August, which I have to get back home in time for, plus the Twins, the Vikings, the Wild—we're known as the state of hockey, did you know that? And what about Paul Bunyan? Heard of him?"

"He wasn't a real person," I said.

"Okay, you want real? Joe Mauer. How about that? Is he real enough for you?" she asked.

"So he won the batting title a few times," I said. "I'll give you that."

"I'm so jealous. My dad and brother, William, are going to the game tonight. They get to be home," she complained. "My dad works for 3M, and he can't leave because he's in the middle of developing a new kind of recycled Scotch tape, and my brother's on this really intense soccer team all summer." She sighed. "Why didn't I think of that?"

"Recycled tape?" I said.

She frowned at me. "Soccer club."

"You play soccer, too?" I asked.

"Well, no. But I'd learn," she said.

"What made your mom want to run for president?" I asked.

76

"She likes helping people," said Emma. "She got really frustrated during the last couple of elections. She felt like no matter what was changing for women and families, too much was staying the same. She was doing really well as governor, so she decided to throw her hat into the ring."

"Which one?" I asked.

"Which . . . ?" She looked confused.

"Hat."

"It's an expression, dummy."

"Never mind," I said. "So what else can you tell me about Minnesota or your mom's campaign? I mean, someone might ask me."

"Well, tons. For instance, this year we're what's called a 'swing state' when it comes to voting, so that's going to work great for my mom," she said.

"You play swing music? You ride swings a lot?" I asked. She didn't say anything, so I kept talking. "What's the difference between swing and battleground? They kept calling Ohio a battleground on the news. And what are normal states called?"

"Normal states are red or blue," she said.

"That makes no sense. Oh, wait. I get it. Red, white, and blue."

"No. There are no white ones." She rolled her eyes. "They either go Democratic, which is blue, or Republican, which is red. But some change back and forth."

"Making them purple," I say.

She shook her head. "Minnesota's usually been blue when it comes to presidents, but lately it's not so predictable. But battleground. That's fought in the trenches."

"We don't have trenches," I said. "And if we did, do you really think your mom would crawl into one?"

"It's a metaphor. Obviously."

"Oh." I was quiet for a minute. "So how come your mom is running as an Independent?" I finally asked. "Couldn't she pick a color?"

"No, because she's always been someone who didn't vote along party lines," Emma said. "Sometimes she was on the Republican side and sometimes the Democratic. She wanted to create a third side."

"Making a square? I mean, um, triangle?" I asked.

Emma gazed at me for a second. "I think I know what my mom should start focusing on." She cracked her gum.

"What's that?"

"Improving schools," she said. "Especially the ones in Ohio."

"Ha-ha," I said. "Very funny." Should I bother telling her that I had been middle-school student of the month back in February? "You know what my clarinet teacher always says?"

"You sound horrible?" she asked.

78

"No. He says flute players are a dime a dozen," I told her.

She narrowed her eyes at me, visibly stung. I smiled at her. So there. She wasn't the only one who could dish it out.

"Well, well, I see you two are getting along swimmingly." Stu suddenly appeared beside me. I jumped. He moved quickly and quietly, like a stealth mouse or something. Up close, his hair was so spiky, it looked like it could cut you if you tried to touch it. "That's excellent, excellent." Stu gently moved my clarinet to the floor and dropped into the aisle seat beside me. "All right. I have a few questions for you, Aidan."

"And so do I." The general appeared, looking down at me.

I felt myself slink down in my seat a little. The general didn't have to do much to intimidate me. Just looking at me would do it.

"First off, how in the world do you actually say Schroeckenbauer?" asked the general, mangling it.

"It's actually pronounced Shrek-en, not Shrocken." I thought about how T.J. called me "Shrieking." Should I mention that? Probably not.

"Okay, okay. Good. Sorry about that," said Stu. "Now, your parents both work for FreezeStar, which is great, real gold material for us. Your older brother is a sports star, and you have a dog. All true?"

"Mostly," I said. "My mom is on leave from FreezeStar, though."

"Right, right. So that's one unemployed parent. No problem. Typical American story." Stu made some notes. "And what kind of dog was that, again?"

"Uh, a mutt," I said. "Her name's Sassafras."

"A mutt, a mutt. Perfect." Stu nodded, then looked up at me. "Any problems with the dog? Has she ever been picked up for biting anyone?" he asked.

"What? No!" I said, wondering why my dog mattered so much.

"Your brother—he hasn't been to juvie or anything. Right?" the general asked.

"Juvie?" I asked.

"Jail for kids," Stu explained.

I could see Emma leaning closer. She probably thought that anyone who wasn't rich like her went to jail. "No, of course not. He's annoying, and he's kind of vain. He's always texting. That's the worst I can say," I told them.

"Fine, fine. Typical American teen," said Stu. "Our team has already done more extensive background checks on you, but I wanted to get your take on things, too. Plus, the more we get to know you, the more fun this will be, right?"

"Right." I coughed, feeling kind of nervous. "So, uh, what do you guys want me to do here?" I asked. "Or wherever it is that we're going?"

Stu shrugged. "No biggie. Just be yourself."

The general raised one eyebrow. "Oh, that can't possibly be enough,"

Emma laughed. But as insulting as the general's comment was, I couldn't help agreeing with him. "Right. Like, shouldn't I do something? Or why am I here?"

"Mm-hm," the general said. "Exactly."

"No worries." Stu patted my back. "There will be a place for you in the Brandon campaign. We'll have to wait a bit and see just what it is."

A sudden, scary thought occurred to me. I was twelve, and Emma, the governor's snooty daughter, was twelve. . . .

I leaned over to the general and asked, "Am I only here just to be friends with her? That's not it, is it? Because we're *not* going to be friends."

"Kid, I have no idea why you're here. If it were up to me, you'd be back home in Ohio, playing baseball. Or trying to, anyway." He chuckled.

"You're the one who came to my house," I reminded him. "You're the one who insisted." Had he already forgotten that?

"Right. Well." He rubbed the back of his neck. "The poll numbers were up, way up. You're an asset to the campaign. You represent middle America. That's a good thing."

"And our numbers are still looking great. We're

still getting tons of hits on our site, linked from your YouTube video," Stu said. "You've gone viral."

"I'm just worried that this is all too temporary," said the general. "We could backslide any second, and did you hear where Flynn is headed today? The Naval Academy. That's a tough image to compete with. Uniforms, flags, naval officers." He shook his head. "We may take a dive after that."

"What about the vice president?" asked Kristen.

"Mathias is visiting a wind farm in Iowa. For whatever that's worth." The general didn't sound impressed. "We've already lost the rabid environmentalists, but we're holding on to the moderates."

"Well, what do *we* have today?" asked Kristen.

Stu quickly checked his BlackBerry. "We're headed to Elyria to a big event sponsored by Ohio Grandmothers for Peace. After that, more appearances in and around Cleveland. And we have a kid with a clarinet that he may or may not know how to play."

"I can play!" I insisted. "You got me on a bad day—that's all."

Neither one of them said anything for a second. Then Stu said, "This is working for us. We're scrappy; that's our image. We're for the little guys. The small businesses, small towns. Middle America."

"People trying to get by, make a decent living, contribute to a greater good through balanced taxes," said the general. "Everyday people. Fairness in work and hiring. Personal freedom."

"Battleground states," I added.

Stu reached over and ruffled my hair. "Bingo! You're getting it, kid. You're really getting it!"

Fine, but I wasn't sure if I wanted to get it. And I definitely didn't want him messing up my hair. It wasn't spiky and he wasn't going to make it that way.

A few minutes later, we pulled up into the convention center parking lot. Secret Service agents got off the bus first to make sure the area was secure.

"So here's what's going to happen," the general said while we waited. "If they ask you what your ideas are, you just keep repeating what you said yesterday." He glanced down at his notes. "The bit about saving jobs and manufacturing."

"Right." What did I say yesterday? I couldn't quite remember, exactly. I must have blocked it out because it was so embarrassing. I guessed I'd been talking about FreezeStar, though. "How one plant closing affects a town?"

"Yes, that. Everyone can relate to that," the general said. "Now, as for the clarinet . . . if they ask you to play, well, that's up to you."

"In that case, I think I'll leave it on the bus," I said. "At least for today."

Stu nodded. "That's just fine. Until we figure out the best way to use your clarinet playing, that's probably the best plan."

"You're going to use it?" I asked.

"We use everything," said Stu. "That's politics. We'll use a cat, a kitten, a grandmother if we have to." He got that wide-eyed, lightbulb-going-off-above-his-head look. "Do you have a grandmother?"

"Sure, I have two of them," I said. "But—"

"Where do they live? Are they mobile?" he asked.

"Sure. Sure they're mobile," I said. "I mean, Grandma E. can't drive at night, and Grammy S. has artificial knees, but—"

"Bionic grandmothers who occasionally need rides. We'll keep that in mind," he said, nodding. "What else you got?"

Kristen looked at her clipboard. "He has asthma," she said.

"Let's use that!" Stu cried. He was so excited about it that I knew he must not have asthma himself.

"Chronic medical conditions are important to Bettina. Very important," the general explained. "She's pushing for universal health coverage, and she's made a lot of changes in her state to make health care more affordable. If elected, she'll continue to fight against the insurance lobbyists and special interests."

I had no idea what a lobbyist was. Someone who hung around lobbies? Was it the same thing as loitering?

"Anything else we should know about your relatives? Uncles? Aunts? Grandfathers?" Stu asked. "If you have any crazy relatives hidden away in an attic, tell us now."

"Huh?" I asked.

He fake-punched me on the arm. "Just kidding. Who was that older guy you were talking to when we pulled into the parking lot?"

"Oh, him? That was Mort. He's definitely not crazy. And he's not a relative, either. But he's kind of like a grandfather to me sometimes." I thought about how we'd sometimes get ice-cream cones after my lesson, and how he gave me ten dollars every year for my birthday.

There were also the times he criticized me and made me play the same measure over and over again. Then he was more like a teacher. A really hard one who never gave out A's.

This was pathetic. I'd only been gone an hour, and I already kind of missed everybody.

"Who's this Mort?" asked Kristen.

"Only the greatest clarinetist Cleveland ever had," I said. "He's my clarinet teacher."

"Oh." She smiled politely. "Well, that's very sweet."

"One last thing, Aidan," said Stu. "Please don't tackle the governor this time around."

"Right. No problem. Not in the cards," I said.

"Then we're set," said Stu just as the lead Secret Service agent got back on the bus. He announced that we were good to go, and everyone got to their feet and started lining up in the aisle.

Kristen glanced back at me. "Don't take this the wrong way, but is that what you're wearing?"

I looked down at my red Ohio State T-shirt, cargo shorts, and sneakers. Wasn't it obvious what I was wearing? "Um . . . yes?"

"Well, uh." She coughed. "Well, it's just that we usually dress kind of nicely for these appearances, so . . ."

"But I'm not even officially appearing, onstage or anything, right? I'm just part of the crowd. Besides, shouldn't I look authentic? Everyone will think I'm a phony if I show up in a suit and tie," I argued.

Not to mention the fact I hadn't brought them. Why didn't they give me a list of what to pack if they cared so much? I didn't even own a suit and tie that fit. I glanced at Emma, to see how I compared. She had on shorts and a T-shirt, too, right?

I did a double take. She was wearing a dress and fancy shoes.

She must have gone into the bathroom and changed

between the time we arrived and now. She was like a superhero with her own personal phone booth. How come she got to look polished and I didn't?

And why did I care? What was happening to me? This campaign was trying to turn me into a dweeb!

Kristen tried to fix the collar of my T-shirt, which was kind of ridiculous since it didn't actually have one. "Maybe we'll have to schedule a shopping trip," she said. "Right after this event."

"Yes, but Aidan has a good point. We don't want anyone to think he's gone all slick," the governor said. "They'd never trust him or believe he was that everyday kid in Ohio."

"Why does he get to wear what *he* wants?" Emma complained.

"Because he's not the potential first daughter," the governor said, "and you are."

"Lucky for me," I said. "That would be awkward."

Emma laughed, but Kristen completely ignored my joke. "We'll tackle your wardrobe issues later," Kristen said. "Right now we need to get out there and meet the crowd!"

"You definitely have issues," Emma said as she pushed past me to be second off the bus, behind her mother.

I stuck out my tongue at her.

"How childish," she commented.

"How rude-ish," I replied.

"That is not even a word," Emma said.

"I know that," I said just as she continued, "Don't you know anything?"

"Kids. Kids! Knock it off. We need a unified front," said the general. "We can't show any weakness here. A weak front is a losing battle. Let's go, everyone! Let's go get those votes! Let's attack from all sides, make sure no one forgets us!" He made it sound like we were landing in France and storming the Normandy coast, or whatever.

As soon as the bus doors opened, a whoosh of hot air—and loud screams—came at me. "Bettina! Brandon! Bettina! Bran-don!" a giant group of fans was chanting. Fresh Idea Party signs were being waved, slogans shouted, pictures snapped.

I felt ridiculous as I stepped off the bus behind everyone else. Who was I, anyway? Just some random kid they picked up along the way. Why was I even here? I could be home watching *Baseball Tonight*.

Well, maybe not, since we no longer had cable.

Maybe I'd somehow end up earning money on this tour, and we could get our cable back when I got home. That would make everyone happy.

Yes. That was it. I'd stick around long enough to get paid. Not that anyone had said anything about paying. I might have to ask about that. There should be a union, just like at FreezeStar.

In the parking lot, reporters were circling the governor within seconds. It was a mob scene, just like the day before, only worse.

"People, people, stand back! Give her some room!" Stu was shouting while the agents and local police kept the crowd at arm's length. The governor was shaking hands and kissing babies while the general urged her forward to the building's entrance. Meanwhile, questions were coming at the governor from all directions:

"What do you have to say about the latest trade deficit numbers?"

"What plans do you have to save the economy?"

"What will the latest immigration act ruling do for migrant farm workers in Ohio?"

"Hot enough for ya?"

I tried to hide in the background, behind Emma. She's taller than I am, so she made a good human shield. I would have to remember that in case the crowd ever turned on us and started throwing tomatoes, cream pies, or worse.

Speaking of which: where *was* my personal Secret Service agent?

"Hey, aren't you that kid?" a reporter came out of nowhere and held a microphone in front of me.

"Which kid?" I asked.

She laughed. "You know, the tackle-first, ask-questions-later kid."

"Um, yeah," I said.

"Oh, yeah, it's him, all right," Emma added.

"I'd love to do an exclusive interview—" the reporter began.

"Hey, look, it's Aidan!" someone else yelled. "The clarinet hero!"

All of a sudden, I had as big a group of reporters around me as the governor had around her, yelling questions.

"How was the bus ride, Aidan?"

"You got any songs for us?"

"Play something, Aidan!"

"What are you doing here?"

I was about to say that I'd been kind of wondering the same thing myself when Stu came to my rescue. "He's the latest Brandonite, of course. His issues are the governor's issues. Now, everyone, if you'll excuse us, we have a rally to attend!"

We headed into the convention center through the back doors. The Secret Service agents and local police escorted us to the backstage area of the convention hall, which reminded me of our school auditorium. The seats were filled, and people were standing in the aisles. Up onstage, a woman from the Ohio Grandmothers for Peace group announced that Governor Brandon was in the building, and the crowd went wild. People were waving Fresh Idea Party banners and American flags. Peeking out from backstage, I saw groups wearing T-shirts that said BRING ON BETTINA! and WE FLIP FOR FIP! There was even a set of twin babies wearing shirts that said, ¡NIÑAS PARA BETTINA!

A group of women in the front row held signs that said, INDEPENDENT WOMEN FOR AN INDEPENDENT PRESIDENT. Onstage, a band started performing a rallying song, while backstage, the governor reviewed her notes one final time.

Stu, the general, and Kristen hovered by the governor, waiting for instructions. Emma stood near me, but we didn't say anything. Finally, a local politician introduced Governor Brandon.

When she walked onstage and said, "Hello, Elyria!" it was like the reaction Christopher's varsity football team gets when they take the field for a big game, only a lot louder. People were screaming, chanting, going a little berserk, if you asked me.

Whoa, I was thinking. She really was growing in popularity. So *this* was what happened when you had a *real* campaign stop in a big city. This was why people got so keyed up over politics. It was like one big party—except for the signs and the weird, gigantic buttons pinned to people's shirts. Fame. Attention. I loved it.

Stu, the general, and Kristen, along with Emma, disappeared into the auditorium to take their reserved seats, leaving me standing there feeling like I'd missed the bus. Why didn't they *tell* me they were going? I didn't know how to sneak around and get past the stage without being seen.

So I was standing backstage listening to the governor's remarks when suddenly someone tugged at my elbow. "Aidan, listen—I know this is last minute, but Stu just told me he changed his mind. They want you onstage," Emma said.

"They do? Why?" I asked. "For what?"

"They want you to stand there and hold this." She gave me a big poster-board sign that said, OHIO LOVES FRESH IDEAS! "You appeal to the Ohio element," she said.

"What?" I struggled to hold on to the large sign.

Emma shrugged. "It's election-speak. That's what Stu told me to tell you. Never mind that. Just go, now!" Emma shoved me hard, the way you'd push a shopping cart if you wanted to hop on and go for a ride in the parking lot. I went flailing and stumbling out of the wings and onto the stage, dropping the poster board.

You know how you try to stop yourself from falling, but it's like slow motion and you can't do anything about it? Instead, you just wave your arms and keep falling. I went careening across the stage and slammed right into Governor Brandon at the podium.

I fell, and I made her fall. It was a domino effect.

I heard the audience gasp. Then nothing, just total, embarrassing silence.

I tried to get up, but my foot slipped and I fell against the bass drum onstage with a giant thump. *"Ba-dum!"*

The drummer peered at me over her drums. Her long beaded braids knocked against the cymbals, sounding like wind chimes. Either that, or I had a head injury that was making me hear tinkling bells.

"You okay, little dude?" she asked.

Man. Even a hippie drummer could insult me.

Governor Brandon, meanwhile, had crashed into a speaker, high heels first.

"Uh, drumroll, please?" I asked. Everyone laughed. When I stood up and shrugged, totally humiliated and wanting to hide, they cheered.

The Secret Service agents just looked at me, shaking their heads as if they couldn't believe I was pulling this stunt again. "Identify the threat," one said to the other.

And he pointed at me. "He is the threat."

The crowd was screaming.

I hurried to help Governor Brandon to her feet. I apologized again for taking her out. She was looking a little flustered and not quite ready to say anything.

I don't know what came over me at that moment, bravery or stupidity, but I stepped up to the mike.

Whoa. There had to be a few thousand people looking at me.

"This wasn't the planned opening for today's speech. And I apologize for that," I said, my voice getting a little louder and clearer with each word. "But when you leave here today, don't remember this clumsy moment of mine. Remember Governor Brandon. You can knock her down," I said, "but you can't count her out!"

There was a deafening roar of applause from the audience as Governor Brandon came up to the mike. She shook my hand as the band kicked off another campaign song. Before she could speak, everyone started chanting her name, and then people onstage began to dance and I backed away, wondering why politicians were such horrible, horrible dancers.

Behind me in the wings, Kristen and Stu were high-fiving each other, only Stu wasn't very coordinated and high-fived Kristen in the eye. So then she was screaming and jumping around, holding her hand over her eye.

I tried to sneak off the stage and back into oblivion. No such luck. Stu and Kristen pushed me back onstage, where I had to sit in a folding chair and listen to Governor Brandon's speech once all the noise died down. I felt like a complete idiot. Also,

I was not all that interested in the speech, which was all about foreign policy and world peace. The Grandmothers for Peace were ecstatic. I was bored.

Next, the governor was talking about human rights, and then about workers' rights and how everyone was entitled to fair and equal treatment.

I was thinking, this is all great, if you *have* a job, but not if you don't and your family has to give up things like name-brand peanut butter, cable TV, and the Internet.

I started thinking, *What would I do if I were in Governor Brandon's shoes (besides look ridiculous)? If I had an audience full of voters to talk to, what would I tell them? Or what would I ask them?*

I remembered something we'd learned in social studies, something that President John F. Kennedy (number thirty-five) once said: "Ask not what your country can do for you—ask what you can do for your country."

I'd modify that slightly.

Ask not what Aidan can do for you—ask what you can do for Aidan. Like, give him back ESPN. And establish a T.J.-free zone.

But that wasn't exactly what President Kennedy was getting at in that famous speech. I knew that it wasn't about being selfish. He was asking people to volunteer, to get involved and help others.

Just then I spotted Emma in the crowd, sitting

next to the general. He might be able to control an army, but he had no control over Emma.

I glared at her. She smiled and waved, as if she were a princess riding on a float in a parade. As if she were completely sweet and innocent and hadn't just pushed me the way, well, the way T.J. would have.

8

"I'm going to get you back," I said, all the while smiling and posing for photos in the lobby of a downtown Cleveland hotel. Was this what being a lobbyist meant?

I'd shaken more hands and smiled more in one afternoon than in the rest of my entire life combined. My face hurt. My mouth hurt. My eyes were so tired that they even hurt. After the event in Elyria, we'd been to every suburb of Cleveland that afternoon, or at least it felt that way. I didn't even know Cleveland *had* that many suburbs—or that people in them would come out to see me. I was just a normal kid from a normal small town. Hadn't they ever met one before? Now we were finishing up a dinner fundraiser that had been held in the enormous ballroom of the hotel where we'd be staying that night.

"Get me back for what?" Emma sounded so sweet and innocent, no one would ever believe she was mean and devious. With T.J., you could tell by looking at him that he was up to something. He'd have this scowl on his upper lip, which was kind of like a smile at the same time, like he was really going to enjoy whatever he was about to say or do to you, and his eyes would narrow, homing in on the target. But Emma acted like she was strolling off to a Niceness Convention. *Then* she punched you in the gut.

"You know what," I said, gritting my teeth. "You pushed me across the stage, back in Elyria." I hadn't even had time to confront her about it because we'd been in public all day. The governor was busy signing autographs and meeting the local FIP leaders who wanted to map out her schedule for the next few days.

"I have no idea what you're talking about. If you have balance problems, that's not my fault," Emma said breezily.

"I don't know how or when, but I will get you back," I said, keeping an eye out for Kristen, or anyone else who'd care how I was talking to Her Royal Pain. "You made a fool out of me on national TV."

"How is that my fault?" She laughed.

"You tricked me, then you shoved me! I wasn't even supposed to be onstage," I said. "You were the one who told me to go, and then you shoved me."

"My pleasure, my pleasure," Emma said. "Love your shirts!" She smiled and waved to a group of young supporters wearing pink BALLERINAS FOR BETTINA T-shirts, who couldn't get close enough to shake her hand. Lucky for them, because who knew what she might do next?

"Are you jealous or something?" I asked. "Because I'm getting so much attention and you're not?"

"Please," she said. "Jealous of you?" Then she turned nice again, telling a woman how much she was enjoying her visits in Ohio. What a phony!

As soon as that group moved on, Kristen pulled us away from the crowd, and we followed her and a couple of Secret Service agents to the elevators.

"I can't wait to get out of these stupid shoes," Emma said, punching the elevator button. "They're killing me. I want to go home."

"You and me both," I said. "You know what? You're so phony. You're going to be a terrible first daughter."

"Not if I can help it," she muttered as we stepped into the elevator. She stood on one side of it, and I stood on the other.

"What?" I asked. That didn't make sense.

"Okay, kids, here's the deal," Kristen said as the door closed. "We've got a little time to unwind before bed. Let's all chill out, put our feet up, have some downtime. No arguing, no fighting, no nonsense."

When the elevator doors opened—with a special key—it turned out that we had the whole top floor to ourselves in one gigantic suite. It was the kind of hotel room you see on TV that only exists in Las Vegas or someplace fancy like that. Only this was Cleveland. And this wasn't on TV, it was real.

"Are we actually staying here?" I asked.

"It's going to be crowded," said Emma. "Can't I have my own room, just once?"

"You always do have your own bedroom." Kristen gave her a stern look. "What's more, I think we can all easily fit here with room to spare."

"Actually, I think we could fit most of Fairstone in here," I said as I followed the two of them around, checking out the spacious suite.

There were several bedrooms branching off a central living room area and a large dining room. A collection of board games was stacked on the coffee table, and a video game console sat next to the large-screen TV and a tower of video games and DVDs. Each bedroom had a private bathroom, and there was a kitchen stocked full of goodies.

"I still say this place is a dump," said Emma as she tossed her shoes onto the floor.

"Yeah, right!" I laughed. It was the nicest hotel I'd ever seen, by a long shot. The only other time I'd stayed in a motel, it was the Lake Erie Lodgette. Christopher and I were there on a guys' fishing trip with my dad, and the only entertainment was a TV with three working channels.

"It is," Emma insisted. She picked up one of the video games and frowned. "This version of *MLB* is two years old."

Our suitcases and other bags had been already delivered to the suite—two giant luggage carts stood just outside the largest bedroom. Kristen got busy unpacking the governor's luggage and started ironing some of her clothes. For every suitcase the governor had, Emma had one, too. Maybe they were going for the best-dressed vote.

I saw my one, medium-size duffel bag with the FreezeStar logo on the luggage cart. It looked like a lunch bag compared to what they'd brought.

Of course, I was a last-minute addition. I wasn't planning on being with these people for weeks on end. You know the whole three-strikes-and-you're-out policy?

I'd knocked down the governor twice now. One more time, and maybe I'd be sent home. I opened the box of Lime Brains that Simon had given me and dropped a couple into my mouth. Would that be so terrible?

"Maybe if you didn't eat so much of that horrible candy, you wouldn't need an inhaler," Emma said from her perch on the desk.

She wasn't nearly as smart as she pretended to be. "You don't know much about asthma, do you?" I asked.

She sniffed and dabbed her nose with a Kleenex. "I have allergies, you know. Serious ones."

"To fun?" I asked.

She glared at me. "I travel with an EpiPen, okay?"

"A what?"

"EpiPen," she said.

"Fascinating. I like pencils, myself," I said.

She sighed. "You're hopeless. It's not a *pen* pen, stupid. It's an injection thing, a syringe. It's just shaped like a pen. If I eat peanut butter or something made with peanuts, I could die," she said dramatically, as if she were going to fall off the desk just thinking about it.

Somehow, I didn't think I would mind that. I picked up the remote control, looking for a sports channel. I hadn't caught the Indians' result from last night's game, and I was dying to know who'd won— it had gone to the thirteenth inning before I finally went to bed.

"Can you quit doing that, please?" Emma asked.

"Quit doing what?" I replied.

"Checking out every channel," she said. "You're driving me nuts."

I laughed. "That's funny."

"What? It's not funny," she said.

"Yeah, it is, because you're allergic to nuts, so if I drive you nuts, you'll be allergic to yourself!" I thought it was pretty brilliant of me to point this out.

She glared at me. Her sense of humor was down in the polls—my poll, anyway. Way, way, way down.

I could tell she was about to go on another tirade when there was a knock at the door. Three knocks, actually, then a pause, then two knocks.

"That'll be the governor." Kristen raced to open the door, nearly tripping over the ironing board.

Governor Brandon walked in, followed by Stu and the general. Her security detail stayed out in the hallway. "Guess what came?" The governor held up a brown box with overnight-delivery stickers all over it.

"My glove!" Emma cried.

"Well, uh, no . . ."

"Mom!"

"I forgot. I'm sorry," the governor said. "We'll buy you one right away. But look!" Governor Brandon lifted a clarinet case from the box. "Now I can play beside Aidan."

"Oh, joy." Emma glared at me.

"I'm going to get changed quickly and then we can see what's what. I have a feeling I'll need some new reeds." The governor disappeared into one of the rooms that branched off the main room of the suite. As soon as she was gone, the general took the remote out of my hand without asking and started clicking through the news channels.

See? Here was another problem. Even when I

did get to watch cable, I had no rights on what to watch—whether I was at home or on the road.

"I have a question," I said.

"Shoot." The general didn't look away from the TV, reading the scrolling headlines at the bottom of the screen.

"Do you ever watch anything but cable news channels?" I asked.

He didn't even take his eyes off CNN. "Why? What would be the point?"

"Well, there are movies. Cartoons. Sports. And you know, other important, normal stuff."

He didn't respond. On the TV, a newscaster was using a SMART Board to illustrate the differences in the latest poll results. "Despite her falls, one candidate is still rising in the polls," the reporter said.

There it was: video footage of my clumsy crash onstage, knocking down the governor. I looked like an out-of-control bowling ball that had taken out several pins.

The general clicked to another news station. They were playing a medley of "Presidential Falls Throughout History," which seemed to feature a lot of President Gerald Ford (number thirty-eight). On yet another station, there was a photo of me and underneath it: BRANDON'S FALL GUY.

"Wow. We've learned something today," said Stu, coming closer, mesmerized.

"What's that?" asked Kristen.

Stu turned to me. "We *need* Aidan. This campaign was in trouble before you showed up. You've got a golden touch."

The general frowned. "I don't know if I'd call it golden. More like bronze. The governor's going to end up with a broken bone if this keeps up. I'm thinking we need to establish a perimeter. You, my friend, will stand outside it."

"But he's effective," said Stu.

"Effective? I think you mean *de*fective," Emma said under her breath, but loudly enough so I could hear her.

Governor Brandon walked into the room, dressed in jeans and a button-down shirt. "So maybe we just need another way for Aidan to be involved. We didn't invite him along to give speeches or dance across stages," she said.

"And now we know why," said Emma, turning on her laptop.

"Ha-ha," I said in a monotone. "Ha."

Emma's mother ignored her. "So, what do you think so far?" the governor asked me. "Everything going all right for you?"

"Sure," I said, nodding. "I guess."

"Is it like you expected?" She sat down in a chair opposite me.

"Um . . . I actually didn't know what to expect," I admitted. "I didn't really have time to expect anything. One minute I was playing in my marching band, and the next thing I know . . ."

"You got sucked into the political machine," said Stu, nodding. "Same thing happened to me. I went to a rally in college, and it changed my life. You can really get swept away when you believe in something. Or someone."

I didn't respond. That wasn't exactly what had happened to me. My experience was more like an alien abduction than being swept away. Now I was on a foreign planet where the only things that mattered were polls and sound bites. I wasn't Stu. I didn't know what I believed in.

"Well. Here we are." Governor Brandon lifted a tray off the table and offered it to me. "Have an oatmeal raisin cookie?"

"Don't bother. He only eats Lime Brains," said Emma in a disdainful tone.

"What's a Lime Brain?" the governor asked me.

"Thank you," I said, taking a cookie off the tray.

"I don't want to know," the general added.

"Sweet-and-sour gummy candy with a crunchy brain middle," I told them.

"Sounds interesting," said the governor.

"Sounds disgusting," added Emma, glancing up from her laptop.

"Well, why don't you have some cookies from your peanut-free stash, Emma?" the governor asked.

"No, thanks, Mom." Emma smiled. "I'm fine."

"Suit yourself. Listen, I had a thought earlier." Governor Brandon set down the tray, put her feet up on the coffee table, and dropped a small cookie into her mouth. "Aidan, you know how your words really got out there, how you made an impact with people?" she asked.

"Yes," I said, and in unison, Stu and the general said, "Yes."

"We were just watching the news about that," Stu said. "Very impressive results."

"Well, we've been wondering," the governor said. "Don't you think maybe it's time for you to speak again?"

"Speak? You mean, in public?" Emma asked. "Him?"

"We'd like to set up some interviews. Tell me what you think. Also, I want you to play," said the governor.

"Play?" I repeated.

She tapped the black case on the table. "Clarinet, what else? Emma, if you want, we can work in the flute. Make this a trio," said her mother.

"Oh, no, not on your life," Emma said under her breath.

"What's that?" her mother asked.

"I was just—it's just that, um, your duet will be better without me." Emma smiled. Why did I get the feeling she was up to something?

"Where exactly would this performance be?" I asked. "At a campaign rally, like today?"

The governor and Stu exchanged awkward glances, as if there was something they didn't want me to know. "Sort of," Stu said.

I didn't like the sound of that. "What does 'sort of' mean?" I asked.

"It would actually be on TV," Stu explained. "Bettina's rolling out her education platform tomorrow, which includes restoring funding for music and other arts. We've gotten her a spot on *Wake Up, America!* She'll be talking about the importance of music education, about how schools are being forced to cut programs and how wrong that is for our future."

That was pretty much what Mort had said. If her issues were Mort's issues, playing clarinet with her would be okay, right?

"She wants to back up her passion for music with some physical evidence. Namely, you," Stu said.

"Oh," I said.

"Go figure," said the general.

I knew that's why they'd asked me to come along. They were only asking me to do what I'd agreed to. So why was I nervous?

"We'll practice together, right now," Governor Brandon said. "If things go well, we can play a duet. If not, there could be a brief, patriotic solo. What do you say, Aidan?"

I looked at Emma. I didn't want to play in front of her. She would mock me; I just knew it. "Uh, is there anywhere we could play that's kind of, you know, more soundproof?" I asked. "Someplace where we wouldn't disturb anyone?"

"Yeah." Emma cracked her gum. "That's what I was thinking."

"These walls are ironclad. I'm not allowed to stay anywhere that isn't practically a concrete bunker," said the governor with a laugh. "No worries."

"Actually, it's more of a, um, focus thing," I said. As in, focus on not being humiliated by Emma. This wasn't good. If I couldn't handle her as an audience, how was I going to deal with however many millions would be watching *Wake Up, America!*?

Kristen turned off the iron and pushed the ironing board out of the way. "Fine, we'll give you privacy. Come on, Emma—let's hit the pool."

"Yes!" Emma jumped up. I'd never seen her move so fast. She'd changed into her swimsuit, and was out the door with Kristen and a Secret Service agent in about two minutes.

Great. She got to go swimming, while I was stuck inside rehearsing with someone who hadn't played the clarinet in forty thousand years. So we could both embarrass ourselves on live TV. That was why Emma had muttered, "Not on your life!"

"I'm headed to the conference room to work on the next speech," Stu announced. "I need to streamline some talking points. You coming?" he asked the general.

"I'm staying put. I've got to get to the root of this kid's appeal," he said as if it made absolutely no sense to him.

After seeing those videos, I kind of had to agree. Although I had sounded cool at the mike. Maybe I was a natural-born public speaker. Everyone has a gift. Maybe mine wasn't clarinet or playing shortstop, the way I'd thought. Maybe it was—

No. That was too boring. I wasn't going through life like these people.

I went into my room and came back with my clarinet. The general took one look at me and pulled a pair of noise-canceling headphones out of his briefcase. He plugged them into the TV and settled back on the recliner to watch.

"So, what do you have for music?" I asked the governor.

"I was counting on you, actually. I'm not sure what Dan put in here. At least he remembered the new reeds I asked for." She sifted through the sheet music in the box. "How about these?"

We practiced for about an hour: Benny Goodman, a Cole Porter piece, some Sousa marches, "The Star-Spangled Banner" and "America the Beautiful," which I played much, much better this time around. I decided not to show her the Mozart music I'd brought along. I didn't think she was up to that, and I didn't want to embarrass her.

The governor wasn't bad. She wasn't good, either, but she wasn't bad. If we practiced some more, we might actually do well at this.

For a few minutes I even forgot where I was. When I'm getting all the notes right, when everything is quiet and I can concentrate, I can go totally inside the music. Sometimes I don't want to come back out.

"That's real playing," Mort had said to me once when I described the feeling to him. "That's what it's all about."

When we had finished playing, the governor looked at me and nodded. "Nice. You have an ear."

"Two of them, actually," I joked.

She smiled. "Musicality, I mean." She told me about her family, how she grew up singing at church. She came from a big family, like Simon's, and all her siblings would get together and sing as a group. "Sometimes I loved it; sometimes I hated it, and it was the last thing I wanted to do. But the thing about music is that it's kind of like public speaking. Learn the skill, and you can go many places with it."

"That's what Mort always says about the clarinet! Learn it and you can learn any wind instrument afterward," I said. "He's my music teacher," I explained.

"You know, I've heard that, too. Clarinet's the most versatile instrument in the world, isn't it? I read that somewhere." She nodded. "You know what, Aidan? It's been so long since I could actually just sit and talk with one person. No microphones."

I sighed. "I know what you mean."

She smiled at me. "Thanks."

"No problem," I said as I started to take apart my clarinet, removing the bell first.

"Don't be nervous about tomorrow. I've been on the show a hundred times," the governor said. "Nicest people in the world."

"I'm not that nervous," I said.

Then I started thinking about it. Everyone I knew watched that show. My parents watched it. Christopher. My grandparents. Simon and his family. Mort. T.J. The entire population of Fairstone. The entire country.

I reassembled my clarinet. "But if it's all the same to you, Governor, I think we'd better keep practicing," I said.

9

That night I couldn't sleep. One, I was extremely nervous about this plan to be on *Wake Up, America!*

And speaking of waking up, our wake-up call was scheduled for five A.M., so we could get to the station at six and go on live at seven-something. What point was there in falling asleep if I had to get up that early?

Two, these days everything I did ended up on TV, anyway, or at least on YouTube. So why did we need to go to *them*?

Three, if I played on TV, I wanted to be really, really, really good. I didn't want to be like the small-town freak show that should have stayed home. I wanted to show everyone that my slip-up on "America the Beautiful" was due to the fact I'd been tackled by Secret Service agents, then frisked and suspected of terrorism. I was better than I'd been that day. Much better. I didn't want Mort cringing when he heard me.

Four, I'd promised to get revenge on Emma. How was I going to do that, exactly?

Whenever I've had trouble in baseball, or learning long division, or the upper register of the clarinet, I've always dealt with it by practicing over and over.

When I was little, I used to say, "If you don't get a success, try, try again." Then Christopher made fun of me, so I switched it to "If at first you don't secede, try, try again."

That also got some laughs, because I got the wording wrong, but that's the thing with me. I don't give up easily.

I pulled on a sweatshirt over my T-shirt, grabbed my clarinet case from beside the bed, picked up a key, and crept out of the room.

I had to find a place that was quiet enough. Maybe a broom closet would work. I could ask at the front desk. Maybe I could use the ballroom, or the exercise room, if no one else was using it at midnight. This hotel was so fancy, it probably had rehearsal space for its guests.

When the elevator doors opened onto the spacious lobby, I was shocked to see Emma lounging on a sofa by the fireplace.

There was a bowl of popcorn on the coffee table beside her, next to a can of soda and a plate of sliced apples with caramel dip.

"What are you doing down here? You're not

allowed to leave the room!" I looked around frantically for Kristen, or a Secret Service agent or two, but didn't see anyone. Were they hiding behind the plants?

"Well, don't tell anyone," she said. "But sometimes I grab a key—"

I was stunned by her boldness. "You get around the Secret Service? I thought that was impossible!"

"Oh, please. I've been around this kind of security forever. They're only human. They have to sleep sometimes, too."

"Yeah, but don't they work in shifts?" I asked.

She shrugged. "All I know is, no one was around. I took advantage." She ate a handful of popcorn. "Why, how did *you* manage to get out?" She made it sound like we'd escaped a maximum-security prison.

I shrugged. "I grabbed a key card that was sitting on top of the TV. It wasn't complicated." I sat down in an armchair. She was watching a baseball game with the sound down low. Not just any game, either: it was the Minnesota Twins against the Cleveland Indians. And the score was tied, in the eleventh inning.

"Well, no, because nobody cares about your safety," she said.

"Thanks," I said. "Thanks a lot."

She laughed. "I just meant—"

"I know you don't care, but some people do. Like

my parents. They're just not here right now," I said.

"I know, I know. I only meant that no one's watching you twenty-four/seven, the way they're watching me," she said. "I can't even go to the bathroom without it being a major security alert."

"Why? What could happen?" I asked. "Do I want to know?"

Her face turned pink. "Nothing."

"What do they think is going to happen to you?" I asked.

"They think I'm going to escape out the window or something. Or get kidnapped, I guess. Since I'm famous. They refuse to let me out of their sight."

"I'd never heard of you before yesterday," I said.

"Well, you probably don't even get cable where you live."

"Well . . . er . . . actually, no. Not anymore." I shrugged.

"What do you mean, not anymore?" she asked.

"We had to give up a few things since my mom's been out of work," I said.

"Oh, sorry. That must be hard." She actually looked nice and sort of honest for a second. "Anyway, have a seat if you want. Chuck over there made me some microwave popcorn, and we tracked down some apples from the breakfast stash." She waved at the clerk working behind the desk. "It's okay, Chuck—he's a friend," she said.

I was? Since when was I a friend?

"So what were you planning? A serenade?"

"Huh?" I asked, distracted by the baseball game.

"Your clarinet." She pointed to the instrument case I was still cradling in my arms.

"I thought I could practice. I couldn't sleep," I said. "But now that I know this is on, forget it. I'll watch this instead."

"The way they hog the TVs up there, you'd never know there was anything *but* news on." She rolled her eyes. "Bo-ring."

"I know, right?" I agreed.

"I can't believe the Twins are losing," Emma said. "The Indians are only the worst team in the AL right now."

"What? They are not!" I said. "The Tigers are way worse."

"Maybe. Not as bad as the Orioles," said Emma.

"Yeah, but they're not in the central division," I said.

"Duh. I know that," Emma said.

"You'll have to cheer for the Nationals soon," I said.

"I hate National League teams. Who wants to see pitchers trying to hit? And have you seen the Nationals' caps? I mean, come on," she said.

"Don't let the reporters hear you say that."

"What?"

"That you hate the National League," I said. "That could be really bad for your mom."

"Do you really want to know the truth? Why I'm down here? I couldn't sleep, either," Emma said, rubbing the side of her face. "I keep thinking about stuff like that. Moving to Washington, if she wins."

"Cool, huh? I'd be psyched if I were you," I said. "Just the buildings—every time I see them on TV, they're so majestic. Or whatever."

She didn't look all that excited about it, which was strange. If I got to move into the White House, I'd have my own room—my own wing—and it would be gigantic. I'd probably have a butler, a maid, and anything in the world I wanted: the latest video games, a decent computer or two, my own *phone*, even.

Of course, I'd hardly ever be home because I'd travel all the time. I'd fly to faraway places, like California and, I don't know, Greece, Egypt, and Spain. I'd see any major-league game I wanted. Forget the cheap seats; I'd have a luxury box. I'd meet the players. I'd throw out first pitches. I'd—

"I hate new stuff," Emma finally said, interrupting my daydream. "I hate being the new kid in school, I don't want to try out for new teams—that is, if they'll even let me try out for new teams, because I might be out of their sight for two seconds chasing down a foul ball—"

"How far foul is it going to be?" I asked. "Virginia?"

She started laughing. "You're funny when you're not being a dork."

We were having fun, until I remembered how she'd thrown me under the bus, or actually, under the drums onstage. "Yeah, thanks. For nothing," I said.

Emma sipped a soda. "So why couldn't *you* sleep?" she asked.

"Haven't you heard? I have to be on TV in the morning. Not just TV—*Wake Up, America!*" Just saying it gave me butterflies. "I have to help your mom convince people to vote for her."

"Yeah. I heard." She passed me the bowl of popcorn. "Is *that* why you brought your clarinet down here?"

"I was going to rehearse, but . . . never mind." The game was going into the twelfth inning, and there was popcorn to eat.

What felt like a few minutes later, someone was shaking my arm. Really strongly. "Aidan! Wake up, wake up!" a voice was saying.

I struggled to open my eyes, but I was so tired.

"What are you even *doing* down here? We looked everywhere for you. Oh, you kids are going to be the death of me!" Kristen cried.

"Kids? Plural? *I* didn't do anything," said Emma, who was beside Kristen.

Kristen began shaking my shoulders. "Aidan, get up. Why are you here and not in your room? You're not allowed to sneak out and sleep in the lobby!"

"Who won?" I rubbed the sleep from my eyes and looked up to see the entire campaign staff standing over me. Emma was dressed for the day, and behind her stood her mother, all ready for our *Wake Up, America!* interview.

Meanwhile, I was wearing my ratty old sweatshirt, shorts, and flip-flops, and hugging my clarinet case to my chest like it was a teddy bear. And I was in public! Except it was the middle of the night, and it was still dark outside. I glanced at the clock above the lobby fireplace. 5:45 A.M. How did it get so early so quickly? Wasn't it just midnight? I glanced over at the front desk, where Chuck was still working.

"You were just here. We were watching the Indians-Twins game," I said to Emma. "Why didn't you wake me up when it was over?"

Emma ignored me. She looked around the lobby. "What's the deal with the breakfast? When does that start? I'm starving."

"Emma, you were right here. It was the twelfth inning," I said.

"I don't know what you're talking about," said Emma. "I wasn't here."

"Yes, you were." I sat up. "You were right here, and Chuck was over there, and we had popcorn—"

"I was in my room the whole night," she said, shooting daggers at me. Then I remembered: she *really* wasn't allowed out at night. Still, I would have liked to have had a partner in crime. Then maybe I wouldn't look so bad.

"You must have been dreaming, kid," said the general. "Come on, I'll follow you back upstairs and wait while you get dressed. You have five minutes." He strode over to the elevator and pressed the up button. "Of course, with your wardrobe, that's more than enough time."

I yawned and stretched my arms, still holding the clarinet. Who even got up at five in the morning? The only other person I could think of who'd be awake was my dad, at work. I suddenly missed him and wished I could call him. He'd know what to say to make me calm down. He'd say, "Whatever happens, it'll be over soon. One way or another."

That was what he said whenever I had to go to the dentist, and it seemed like this TV show could be about as unpleasant.

"FYI, the Twins won it in fourteen," the general said. "Indians had a chance to win, but that new closer—what's his name?"

"Hayashi?" I said.

"Right. He gave up a three-run homer in the bottom of the fourteenth inning," the general told me. "Course, the Twins only needed two runs to win it. *Sayonara*, Indians."

"Great. Just great," I said as we stepped into the elevator. Even my heroes were letting me down.

10

"Haircut, fix Aidan's hair," the general said as we pulled up in front of the TV studio in downtown Cleveland. "I told you we should have had it cut."

"Why is that my job?" Stu stopped. "Fine, I'll do it." He rummaged in his shoulder bag and came up with a tube of hair gel.

"I wouldn't worry about it, Stu," the governor said. "They're probably going to whisk you into hair and makeup as soon as we walk in, Aidan."

"Aidan's not supposed to look perfect," Emma said. "Remember? You're supposed to look authentic. And you do. You look authentically awful."

"What are you talking about?" I said. "This is my best Mud Hens shirt." The Toledo Mud Hens are a Triple-A affiliate team of the Detroit Tigers, and the only team whose games I actually get to see in person. I had on a pair of decent jeans and my usual sneakers.

The elevator doors opened, and I stepped off beside her. "It's your fault I didn't have time to get ready this morning like everyone else," I said quietly. "And you know it."

"*I* didn't make you come downstairs in the middle of the night," she whispered back. "*I* didn't force you to watch that baseball game. So if you're looking for someone to blame for your bed head, it's not me."

"You could have said something," I whispered. "When you left."

"And wake you up from your beauty sleep?" she asked. "No way."

In the lounge outside the recording studio, where guests waited, there were comfy chairs, a large TV, and a breakfast buffet. I reached for a banana muffin.

Kristen grabbed my arm and nearly tore the muffin out of my hand. "You can eat afterward, not before."

"But I'm hungry," I said.

"Yes, but you're going on in five minutes. You won't have time to brush your teeth again. Interview first, eat second," she said as if it were something everyone in the world knew except me.

"She's always saying that." Emma looked at me, rolled her eyes, then picked up a bunch of grapes and popped a few into her mouth.

"Hey! What about her?" I asked.

"She's not going on camera this morning. You are," said Kristen.

"So there." Emma picked up a chocolate donut and took a bite. "Mm, oh, that's delicious."

"What about your peanut allergy?" I asked.

"Don't worry, this is all peanut-free," said Kristen. "I had it all arranged ahead of time, like always."

"Too bad," I muttered. Not that I wanted to see Emma seriously hurt or anything, but after what she'd done to me, a little choking fit wouldn't be horrible, would it?

The governor and I practically flew in and out of the hair and makeup room. Even then, it was too much time. Maybe my hair needed a little fixing, but since when did I need makeup? I hoped no one watching would notice. I'd never be able to live that down.

"Kind of weird wearing blush, isn't it?" the governor asked, looking over at me from her seat, eyes half closed as they dabbed makeup onto her lids.

"I wouldn't know," I said.

The makeup artist swished a brush against my cheeks. "Well, now you do," she said.

"Great. Just great," I mumbled, avoiding the mirror in front of me.

Then a local producer walked us out to the set, where TVs in every direction showed the *Wake Up, America!* broadcast in progress.

"Looking good, kid," Stu said, nodding at my styled hair.

"Is that powder on your face?" the general asked.

"Leave me alone. This wasn't my idea," I grumbled in reply.

The producer told me and the rest of the campaign team how everything would happen, and in what order. I found out we were going to be interviewed by the superstar host, Candace McKnight, via satellite. We'd talk to her on-screen, sort of like Skyping. I did that with my grandparents sometimes, so I was used to it.

We'd sit on a sofa to talk first, then move over to where they'd set up chairs and music stands so we could perform our duet. The show was filmed live in New York City, but they would hook up with their affiliate station here to interview us.

"And in just a few minutes," Candace was saying to the TV audience—all however many millions of them, "we'll be live with the latest sensations on the presidential campaign trail right now. We'll be right back with the candidate and the clarinet player!"

The camera at the New York studio panned to the large plate-glass window behind Candace's desk, where people were holding up signs. My eyes widened as I saw what they said:

WE LOVE AIDAN

CLARINETS RULE!

127

SHORT HAPPENS

Sure, the last one was kind of insulting. But I just stood there with my mouth hanging open. "They know who I am in New York?" I asked. "New York ... City?"

"Buddy, it's what we've been trying to tell you," Stu said. "You're a media magnet."

"One minute till airtime," a voice said over the PA system. "Governor Brandon, Aidan Slockenbeamer, on set please."

"Schroeckenbauer," I said. "It's not that hard to say!"

I hustled out to the set. The governor was already perched on the sofa. Emma was sitting in a canvas-back director's chair, off camera. "Break a leg!" she said cheerfully as I walked past her.

"What?" I nearly tripped on all the electrical cords running across the floor. Did she have a death wish for me or something?

Our clarinets were laid out on the desk on the side, along with our sheet music on a couple of stands. I flashed a nervous smile at the governor, then took a seat beside her on the sofa.

"You'll be fine," she assured me, scooting over a bit. She pursed her lips, and smiled at the camera. "*We'll* be fine."

Suddenly, the host from *Wake Up, America!* was

looking back at me from a TV screen. Candace McKnight was extremely pretty, with perfect hair. I was supposed to talk to *her*? Now? I felt my mouth go completely dry. Over the loudspeaker, a voice was saying, "Ten . . . five . . . three, two, one, and we're live!"

"And now we go to Cleveland," Candace McKnight said, "where we're checking in with presidential candidate Governor Bettina Brandon at our affiliate station. She's traveling all over the central Midwest on the Fresh Idea bus, campaigning for the Fresh Idea Party. Good morning, Governor."

"Good morning, Candace!" the governor said, smiling.

"How's the weather in Cleveland this morning?" Candace asked.

"Lovely. You know, we're having a great time, meeting lots of new people, and getting new ideas out there," the governor said.

"That's wonderful. We could use some new ideas here at *Wake Up, America!*" Candace said.

"I don't know about that, Candace. Your show is a well-oiled machine. I think you're doing everything right," the governor said.

"We'll take the compliment, thanks," said Candace. "Now, I understand you've brought a friend and campaign worker along to talk to us this morning. Aidan Shriekenhoffer, nice to see you." She smiled at me.

"Thank you. It's, uh, nice to be here." I decided not to correct her pronunciation of my last name. There just wasn't enough time to tell everyone in the world how it was actually said or spelled. I yawned.

"Did we wake you up?" she asked.

"Oh! Sorry, sorry," I said. "Campaign work keeps me up late at night."

"That would explain the *hair*," Emma said off camera, but loudly enough for everyone to hear.

Out of the corner of my eye, I saw Kristen urge Emma out of the chair near the set and lead her farther away from us.

"Campaigning like this may be exhausting at times," the governor chimed in, "but it's also exhilarating. There's nothing like meeting people from all over this great country who inspire me to keep working hard for them. If I'm elected, I'll work tirelessly to make sure people's rights, homes, and jobs are protected."

I yawned again. I felt bad, but I couldn't help it! This time I covered my mouth and coughed, hoping to hide it.

"So Aidan, turning to you now," Candace said. "As you said, back when all this began, the biggest issue you see facing the country is job security. Is that right?"

Was that it? "Sure." I nodded. "Yes."

"And why was that, for those of our viewers who

might not have seen you yet?" she asked. "Of course, you'd have to be living under a rock not to have seen you." She laughed. "But—anyway, go ahead."

I smiled, and felt myself blushing a little. "Well, I come from a town where there's basically one big company, and everything kind of relates to that company somehow. They sponsor lots of things in our town, like Little League, the music program. Basically, they keep us going. My dad works there," I said. "And my mom used to until she got laid off. And my grandfather did, too, and maybe I'll end up working there, if it's still around."

"And that's the issue," Governor Brandon said, joining the conversation. "Will important manufacturing jobs still exist here in the U.S. by the time Aidan enters the workforce? Only if we're willing to make an investment in the manufacturing sector. As president, I'll work to create tax breaks for industries—"

"Excuse me, Governor," Candace said. "I'd like to follow up on something Aidan mentioned. Aidan, you said your mother used to work for the town's main employer until she was laid off. Isn't that one of the issues here? Growing unemployment?"

"Yes, we need to create an economy—" the governor began.

"Aidan?" Candace interrupted her again.

I glanced at the governor, and she nodded for me to go ahead. "Well, yeah," I said to the camera. "My mom lost her job and we had to give up cable, Internet, trips to Cedar Point. We're eating spaghetti, like, five nights a week."

"Don't you like spaghetti?" asked Candace. "I heard it's one of your favorite foods."

"Well, sure," I said, wondering how she would know that, "but everything gets old after a while. Like being out of work. Maybe at first you get to watch a bunch of TV or relax and read a book. But then it's not vacation anymore, you know? It's definitely not the same thing as vacation. That's what my mom says, anyway. She really wants to go back to work, but she just can't."

"That's an interesting point," said Candace. "Well, I have another question for the Brandon campaign. First of all, are you aware of this?" She used the SMART Board on set to call up a Facebook page. "There's a movement on Facebook," she said. "A whole lot of people want you to pick *him* as vice president."

"Pick him who?" I said.

"You, Aidan." Candace tapped the board and made the type and images larger. There was a picture of me—my school picture from the year before—and the page was named SUPPORT AIDAN FOR VP!

"There are over ten million members of this

group," Candace said. "What's your reaction? Governor Brandon? Aidan?"

My mouth was hanging open. I was shocked. Then I was flattered. Then I burst out laughing. "It's not like that can actually happen, right?" I said to the governor. I was pretty sure you had to be at least old enough to vote to be elected to anything.

"Well, I think this reflects what voters are looking for in this election cycle," said the governor. "They want people who tell it like it is, who aren't afraid to put the big issues on the table and talk about them, and come up with fresh solutions to old problems."

Man, she was good at talking on the spur of the moment. She didn't even seem nervous. She'd probably make a great president, I suddenly realized, based on that fact alone.

"Aidan? What's your take on being chosen for vice president?" asked Candace. "Why do you think so many voters are behind this?"

"Um . . . people like the clarinet?" I said. Everyone in the studio laughed. "What?" I said. "It's true."

"True enough," Candace agreed, nodding. "In that case, why don't you play a little something for us? I understand you and the governor have a duet in mind. When we come back from break, we'll hear from Governor Brandon and the clarinet hero! And later, how to save money on a home loan, plus hosting the perfect barbecue with Chef Marietta!"

As soon as we were off the air, the governor and I scrambled to get ready. We stuck our reeds in our mouths, and got our music stands set up at the right heights, while a technician checked the mikes. Everything was in order. We were ready.

Except that when we looked at our sheet music, it wasn't sheet music at all. It was a room-service menu. I was so hungry that I started scanning it without even meaning to.

EGGS BENEDICT ~ $19.99

PASTRY PLATE ~ $18.99

FRESHLY SQUEEZED ORANGE JUICE ~ $7.99

"Eight bucks for orange juice?" I said. "Are they serious?"

"Welcome back, America," Candace was saying, somewhere far away, while I thought about getting bacon, eggs, waffles, and orange juice.

"How did this get in here?" asked Governor Brandon. "What happened to our—to our— It must be here somewhere...."

"Governor, Aidan?" Candace was saying while I frantically sorted through our cases for something, anything we could use. I could just imagine the headline: *Disorganized Governor Could Never Be President. Lost Music Leads to Lost Race.*

"We have a little snag in the plan," the governor said. "Somehow our music didn't make it from the hotel room to the studio. I'm not sure what happened." She looked at me, a little bit panicked.

I didn't know what was going on, but I wasn't going to let this one mistake bring down her candidacy. This was a minor snafu. After she'd been so nice to me and my town, I could handle this for her.

"You know what? It's my fault, Candace," I said. "I'm sorry. It was my job to have the music ready, and as you said, I'm a little tired. I guess instead of grabbing our sheet music, I picked up this menu instead."

"Oh." Candace laughed, then looked a little confused, as if she wasn't sure how she was going to fill the next few minutes of airtime. "Well, can you play, uh, Eggs Benedict for us?" she joked.

I smacked my forehead with the menu. "I can't believe I did that. What an idiot, huh? But I can play something from memory. Would that be okay?" I asked.

"Could you? Really?" The governor looked as happy as if I'd just told her she'd won the November election. As if she were floating in the ocean, about to sink, and I'd just thrown her a life preserver.

"That would be perfect," Candace said. "Ladies and gentlemen, the clarinet hero, live in our Cleveland studio. Hit it, Aidan!"

I smiled at the camera, then launched into "The Star-Spangled Banner."

In a way, everything goes back to baseball. When you want to avoid a squeeze play, you bunt.

"Aidan, you were great! I can't thank you enough." Governor Brandon gave my shoulder a squeeze as we walked off the set five minutes later, post-national anthem and post-interview. "You really know how to come through in the clutch."

"Thanks. It's no problem," I said, relieved this performance had gone way better than my last. "I've been playing that since fourth grade."

"I didn't mean that," she said. "I meant how you covered for me on national TV. Did you hear everyone cheering in New York when you were done?"

"Now that's what I call a fluff piece," the general complained backstage as the producer unclipped our mikes.

"Fluff nothing," said the governor. "We got all my ideas across and then some. And wasn't Aidan terrific?"

"Yes. He was," the general grudgingly admitted. "But that whole Facebook movement is ridiculous. I mean, is the American public that dumb? Don't they know you have to be thirty-five to hold office?"

"It's called having fun. You should look into it," Stu told him. "Here, Aidan. Your mom's on the phone. I called her to make sure they knew you'd be on and we've been chatting for a while," he said. "She has a lot of questions for you. A lot." He handed me his BlackBerry.

"Mom?" I said, edging away from the crowd so I'd be able to hear her.

"You were great, honey!" my mom cried. "You were fantastic—everyone in town was watching you. You looked tired, though. Have they been working you too hard? Have you been eating enough? I know you don't like to try new foods, and I wanted to make sure they're getting you things you like. Have you been drinking enough milk?"

"Mom, I'm fine," I said. I'd only been gone twenty-four hours—not even—and she had a million questions.

"Are you sure?" she asked.

"Yup," I said. "I overslept—that's all. I stayed up late watching the game last night."

"Is it true that they want you to be vice president? Oh, can you just imagine?" Mom sounded a little delirious.

"Mom. It can't actually happen," I said.

"Yes, I know, but just the thought that people

want it to happen. And with my favorite candidate, too! Oh, I'm so proud of you, I could just burst."

"Mom, calm down," I said. "Hey, did Dad get to watch?"

"No, but we had your grandparents record it for him on their DVR," she said. "Aidan, do you know anyone else who's ever been on national TV and had people hold up signs for them? You're magnetic. You're special. It's like I've been telling you for years. Height doesn't matter. Personality does."

"Right, okay, Mom, whatever." She was starting to embarrass me.

"Hear that, shrimp?" Christopher asked, getting on the phone. "Being short is okay as long as you score us tickets to live in D.C. for the next four years!"

"Thanks, Christopher. Listen, I have to go now. Stu needs his BlackBerry back," I said. "Important calls to make. Bye, everyone!"

"It's okay, you could have talked longer," Stu said as I returned his phone to him.

"I know, but my brother was insulting me," I said. "It's nothing new, but I didn't exactly want to get into it with him." As much as I kind of missed Christopher and everyone at home, I'd been enjoying being somewhere on my own for once. It was a little bit scary at times, but I also liked it. Besides, I had something I wanted to ask Emma. "Where's Emma?" I asked.

"Green room. Why don't you go find her and have some breakfast? We'll be moving on soon, and I'll go check in with the general and Bettina, see what the plan is. Stay there—do not leave," Stu told me.

"Right," I said.

I found my way back to the green room. It was easy to find, what with the security posted outside the door, protecting Emma.

She was sitting alone in the corner, on the sofa. She looked up at me, and her face was streaked with tears. Emma? Crying? She didn't strike me as the crying type.

She quickly brushed her face with the sleeve of her sweater. "If Kristen was here, she'd tell me not to do that," she said.

"Probably," I said. That reminded me: I need to clean my own face, get rid of all that beige and pink makeup stuff. I grabbed a napkin, wet it with water, and scrubbed my face. "What's up?" I asked Emma.

"What do you think is up? My mom's poll numbers. Her chances at becoming president. You know, I thought you could handle this, but I can see I'll have to do more myself," she said.

"What?" I asked, tossing the makeup-streaked napkin in the trash. I moved on to the food buffet and started filling a plate with pastries.

"You weren't supposed to play well," Emma said. "You weren't supposed to be funny like that, and sleepy, and come to the rescue."

"I wasn't?" I asked, mid-bite of a cinnamon roll.

"No! I was counting on you to mess up!" she said. "That's why I gave you a menu instead of your music. But you messed up at messing up." She threw up her hands. "Can't you do anything right?"

11

"What? You're the one who stole our music?" I asked. "That could have been a disaster!"

"I know! It was supposed to be. You were supposed to make a fool out of my mom, not make the country like her even more," Emma continued. She glanced at the door, ran over, and pressed her ear against it.

"I don't get it," I said.

"Of course you don't." She sighed, exasperated. "You messed everything up for me. I only suggested you come along on this dumb bus tour so that you could ruin the campaign, not save it."

"This was your idea?" I shook my head. "No way. It was the Haircut's idea."

"No, it wasn't. The Haircut agreed with me, but I thought of it first," Emma insisted. "I don't want her to win. Isn't it obvious?"

"Obvious? Why wouldn't you want her to win?" I asked. I finished the cinnamon roll and moved on to a raspberry Danish.

"Have you seen what happens to first daughters? Do you have any idea?" she asked. "You have to dress nicely all the time. You have to go to private school. You can't go anywhere without a bunch of security people hounding you. Wherever you go, the media follows you. Everyone wants to go to your wedding. You could even end up on a show like *Dancing with the Stars*." She shuddered.

"Are you really worried about all that now?" I said. "Already? She's only *running* for president; she hasn't won yet."

"No, but if things keep going the way they are . . . she'll probably write a book about me. A children's book. Everyone will love it and be like, 'Oh, Emma's so cute,' except I'm not cute, and I don't want to be that girl. We'll have to wear matching outfits to the inauguration; we'll have to stand outside and freeze; we'll have to—"

"Have to what?" I asked. "Travel, see the world, have every opportunity—"

"Yes, but in matching outfits!" she cried.

"I think you have that wrong," I said, trying to remember if I'd ever watched an inauguration. "You're thinking of Christmas pictures and junk like that."

"Still!" she cried. "Isn't that bad enough? When we met you, I figured you'd be the perfect person to ruin my mom's chances. You were supposed to be horrible for the campaign, a downright disaster. Not make her even *more* popular."

I tried to think how I would feel if my mom were running for office, if she had a shot of becoming that important or that famous. I couldn't imagine what it'd be like. "Well, I think you should try to look on the bright side," I said.

"What bright side?" Emma asked in a flat voice.

"All the good things about living in Washington, D.C.!" I said.

"Have you ever lived there?"

"No, but—"

"Well, then, how do you know?" Emma cried. "And what about moving away from all my friends? Never being able to play baseball or other sports again? Never being on a team? Never just going down the street to get an ice cream?"

"It wouldn't be 'never,'" I said. "Just four years."

"It might be eight!" Emma said. "Look how popular my mom's getting. By the time she leaves office, I'll be in college. And you know who would follow me to college? Secret Service. Paparazzi. Reporters. Do you have any idea how much I hate having my picture taken?"

"But you're so good at it," I reminded her. "You always smile."

"I'm faking it. Duh." She rolled her eyes.

"Oh. Well, what about the fact this is something

your mom really, really wants? Doesn't that count?" I asked. I reached for a bottle of orange juice and unscrewed the cap.

"Sure. I'm all for her being governor. Don't get me wrong," Emma said. "But this national stuff? I mean, would you like to spend a couple weeks of your summer campaigning on a bus?"

I swallowed the juice and said, "I *am* spending part of my summer with the campaign."

"Well, don't worry. You'll be gone soon," she said.

I gulped, nearly choking on my next sip. "What's that supposed to mean?"

"You'll screw up for real, and the same thing will happen to you that happened to me. Watch. You think *you* had a bad YouTube moment?" She handed me her iPhone. "Check this out."

She showed me a video of a pep rally for her mom, early in the spring. Emma was standing onstage behind the governor, not paying attention. Then she started making goofy faces at someone in the crowd. When her mom invited her up to the mike to say something, she opened her mouth and let out a loud, very disgusting burp.

Her mom looked like she wanted to sink into the floor and never come out again.

"Wow. A million and a half views. Talk about viral," I said.

"I know. It was awful, and Mom's been trying to live it down ever since. I'm too much of a 'live wire.' They actually think I did it on purpose!" she said.

"Well, did you?" I asked.

"No. Well, maybe. Anyway, that's beside the point. My dad and my brother get to be at home, but I have to be out here reforming my image. They go swimming, play baseball, go out for ice cream, hit the amusement park. But I have to go to luncheons. I finally figured out what that means. Lunch that lasts an eon," she said. "I miss my friends. I miss my room. This whole campaign is ruining my life."

"So instead you set me up to ruin the campaign. Why don't *you* do it?" I asked.

"I tried, okay? And I got put in Miss Hartford's Country Day School for Girls," she said. "I got a whole new wardrobe of dresses and sweaters. I used to dress like *you*."

What was she talking about? "Like me? Really?"

She considered me and my outfit. "Well, no. Not that bad."

My face started to burn.

"But I used to wear normal clothes, not party clothes," Emma went on. "I didn't have to style myself or have Kristen approve my outfit every day. There's nothing wrong with purple hair, not when it's crazy hair day at Miss Hartford's Country Day School."

I didn't know how to tell her this, but I really didn't care about her clothes *or* her hair. "I don't have any sisters," I blurted out.

"Oh, I know," she said. "I know everything about you."

"You do?" I asked.

Emma nodded. "I've been doing research. If things don't go right for me, you'll find out about it."

"Are you . . . ? Wait a second. Are you threatening me?" I asked. It wasn't as if I didn't know what that sounded like. T.J. had threatened me lots of times. "Are presidential candidates' kids supposed to go around threatening people?"

Suddenly, there was a knock at the door. "You guys all set?" Kristen asked, poking her head inside. "Did you get enough to eat? The bus is ready to roll."

I followed Emma, and we headed back to the lobby, where a few reporters were still hanging around, even though it seemed as if everyone important, like the governor, had already left. They swarmed to me and Emma like bees around an open can of Coke.

"So, Emma, what do you think about your friend Aidan here running for vice president?" one of them asked.

"We're not taking any questions," Kristen said, trying to get between the microphone and Emma.

"No, it's okay," Emma said. "Him for vice

president?" She pointed at me and laughed. "For one thing, it's impossible. For another, he dresses pretty badly to be vice president."

The reporters laughed and struggled to get even closer to her. Emma looked a little penned in, like a wild animal when it's captured. Her right eye started to twitch. The pressure was really getting to her—the pressure of trying to bring down her mother's campaign, that is.

"I'm just saying, not everyone is how they seem," she said in a sweet voice. "Some people have skeletons."

I stepped up. "We all have skeletons," I said, wishing I could just tell everyone the truth about Emma. "That's what bones are."

"Not like that, you idiot," she said under her breath. Then she smiled sweetly for the reporters again. "We'll just have to see what happens in the next few days. I'll leave it to my mother to talk about her *real* pick for vice president."

"That's enough for now," Kristen said, pulling Emma toward the exit.

Emma entered the revolving door and spun through it to the outside.

I tried to follow her, but she jammed the door with her foot and kept me from turning it. I stuck out my tongue at her. I'd had enough of being set up to look like a fool. If she thought she was going to use me to sabotage her mom's campaign, she was wrong. I wasn't going to ruin it for her. Governor Brandon hadn't done anything to hurt me, and besides, my mom was a big fan of hers—and I was becoming one, too.

If Emma wanted to bring down the Brandon campaign, she'd have to find some other way.

12

"You slept through Fort Wayne."

I rubbed my eyes and looked at Emma. Why was I sleeping on the bus?

Oh. Right. I'd stayed up too late at the hotel the night before, watching a movie, after campaigning all day following our *Wake Up, America!* appearance. After Cleveland, we'd visited Youngstown, Akron—I was actually losing track of all the stops we'd made. Then I'd had to get up early, have a campaign breakfast, and start all over again. This morning we'd already been to Mansfield, Westerville, and Lima—all towns in Ohio that I kind of knew. If everyone in Ohio didn't know about Governor Brandon by now, I'd have been surprised.

I had cousins in Lima, but I didn't see them in the crowd, or they didn't see me. They were second cousins and I hadn't seen them in a while.

"Why didn't you wake me up for Fort Wayne?"

I asked. I'd never spent much time in Indiana, even though it was so close, and I was curious.

Emma shrugged. "My mom wanted you to sleep. She said being on the campaign trail had worn you out."

"So now what?" I asked. "Where are we going?"

"Some county fair. It could be fun," Emma said. "Of course, it won't be *nearly* as good as the Minnesota State Fair."

I glared at her. I'd had more than enough of her bragging about Minnesota. I wasn't going to talk to her any more, now that I knew that she'd only wanted me to come on the trip so she could make me ruin it for her mom. What kind of person did that?

She'd set me up more than once. First she'd pushed me onstage. Then she'd let me sleep on the sofa. Then she'd stolen my sheet music. I had so many things to get her back for that I was losing count.

I didn't trust her. And when exactly was I supposed to tell Governor Brandon that her daughter was dead set on smashing her successful campaign to pieces? And that she'd sort of hired me to do it?

Should I just try to leave quietly and let them figure it out on their own?

Or should I stick around and try to counteract every move Emma made, because her mother had been nothing but nice to me and didn't deserve to be sabotaged?

And why was I sleeping when I needed to figure this all out?

"When are you going to tell your mom what you're up to?" I asked.

Rats. I'd already forgotten that I wasn't talking to her.

She narrowed her eyes. "Never. Why?"

"Why don't you just be honest with her and tell her how you feel, that you don't want to go to Washington?" I asked.

"Please. Like she'll listen to that?" scoffed Emma. "She's always saying how history compels her to run for president. What am I going to do, fight history?"

"I don't know," I said. "If it were my mom . . ."

"Would *you* tell her you didn't want to move to the White House?" asked Emma.

I had to think about it for a minute. First I had to imagine my mother as a presidential candidate. Before that I had to picture her as a governor. I couldn't see her getting excited about either— but then again, she did make an excellent PTA secretary. Maybe she had dreams I didn't know about.

If she did, would I get in the way of them?

"It's hard to put myself in your shoes," I admitted.

All of a sudden, the bus jerked to a stop. Then it started. Then it slowed down and stopped again. We were stuck on the highway, in a traffic jam.

"Aidan. Aidan! You've got to get up here. Hurry!" shouted the governor.

Why would she need me? Clarinet emergency? I wondered as I hurried up the aisle toward the sofa area up front.

"Look!" She pointed out the bus window at a car that was stopped just in front of us. On its bumper was a neon-yellow bumper sticker that said, BRANDON/ SCHROECKENBAUER: A FRESH IDEA FOR AMERICA.

Emma stood beside me and stared out the window. "That's one long bumper sticker," she said.

"Well, would you look at that?" Stu grinned from ear to ear.

"Who has even had time to make bumper stickers?" asked the general. "We just met this kid a few days ago."

"Politics move quickly, especially in an election year," Stu said.

"I know that, Haircut," said the general. "I've been working in politics since you were in diapers."

"We only learned about it this morning," said the governor. "And there are already bumper stickers? It's kind of ridiculous, how far people want to take this Facebook idea," Governor Brandon said.

"Yeah, no kidding," added Emma.

"Obviously, it can't be done," said Governor

Brandon. "But is there a way to make people think that it *is* being done?"

Stu's forehead creased in confusion. "How do you mean?"

"Well, half of politics is perception, right? So maybe we should act like we're considering it," said the governor.

"Bettina." The general coughed. "With all due respect. That's not only impossible; it's insane. It will make you seem like you don't know what you're doing. We're not doing that. Let's get back to your VP list and make some calls."

"Right. Of course." Governor Brandon shook her head and laughed at the same time. "I think I've been on the campaign trail too long. It's starting to get to me."

"Maybe you need to take some time off," Kristen said. "Take a break from campaigning for the day. Get a manicure, a massage—"

"Wouldn't that be nice?" Governor Brandon replied with a sigh.

"Hello? What are you talking about?" the general roared. "The pundits would accuse you of doing your nails while terrorists plotted, of putting personal happiness above the country's needs—"

"I get it, General," said the governor. "I wasn't saying I'd do it. It's just nice to think about."

The bus driver got out of his seat and stood

in the aisle, facing us. "Well, looks like we're going to be stopped here for a while," he said. "A truck overturned—sounds like it was headed to Elkhart County Fair, too. Apparently, there are pigs wandering on the road up ahead. We can't move till they're all corralled."

The general got to his feet, looking excited. "Pigs on the loose? Are you thinking what I'm thinking?" he asked Stu.

"Photo op!" Stu cried. "Let's run, before they all get caught!"

"Come on, Kristen. You can fix my hair while we run. Emma, Aidan, stay on the bus!" the governor ordered us. "Don't get off under any circumstances! It's not safe!"

And just like that, Governor Brandon, her campaign workers, and a team of Secret Service agents got off the bus and were hustling down the side of the road, meeting and greeting voters in every car and mingling with lost pigs.

"Why is it not safe for us but okay for them?" I asked as we gazed out the front window at all the activity.

"Because we're kids. And kids can't do anything," said Emma. "Especially me." She sighed. "I could be swimming right now. I could be playing basketball, or hanging out with my friends. I'd even take homework over this."

"Wow. That's extreme," I said.

She drummed her nails against the top of the head rest. "Not really. I love school."

"Yeah. Me, too," I admitted. I knew the cool thing was to pretend that I didn't, but what point was there in studying hard and not owning up to it? It'd be like batting .400 and keeping that a secret. Nobody would do that.

"Did you ever read *Charlotte's Web*?" Emma asked.

"Of course. What do you take me for, a total imbecile?" I said. "Wait. Don't answer that."

"Remember when they went to the fair, and you were afraid Wilbur was going to die, but Charlotte died instead?" Emma asked.

"Yeah. Kind of." I'd cried the night I finished the book. But I wasn't about to tell her that.

We were totally alone except for the driver. There were no campaign workers in sight; they were all with the governor. Because of the quickly moving situation, all the Secret Service had gone with the governor, too. If Emma wanted to run away, or do something while everyone's attention was on her mother and not her, this was her chance.

"You want to play catch, or what?" she asked.

"Sure. But you don't have a glove," I said.

"Mom finally got someone to go buy me a new

one yesterday," she said. "She couldn't argue because baseball is exercise and that's part of her stupid kids' plan."

"She has a plan for stupid kids?" I asked.

She ignored me and tiptoed down the aisle. We looked around outside for the driver and spotted him standing beside the bus, on the driver's side. We quietly stepped off the bus and went down the grassy bank.

We started to toss the ball back and forth. I wasn't trying to throw it my hardest, but after being cooped up for the past few days, my arm was itching to do something. I heard a snap as the ball hit Emma's glove.

She tossed it back with equal force, the ball zinging into my glove. She could throw almost as hard as T.J. That was a compliment, but I wasn't sure she'd take it as one.

I thought about T.J. and threw the ball back even harder. I saw her wince as she caught it. Then she tossed it back to me, a line drive that smacked into my glove with a crack.

She wasn't bad at all. I'd only seen her throw and catch so far, but I had a feeling that if she lived in Fairstone, she'd be one of the better players on the girls' Little League team. I was about to tell her that when I remembered how she had set me up to ruin the campaign.

Instead, I hurled the baseball back to her. Then she flung it back to me. Then back and forth, each time throwing harder, as if we were trying to turn double plays right there beside the bus.

Suddenly, she said, "Ouch!" and I saw her rubbing her palm. She walked closer to me. "Look, let's not kill each other with the baseball."

"Okay," I agreed. "What should we use?"

"Light sabers?" she suggested.

"Light sabers?" I said.

"Well, they'd be less painful. Until the saber pierced your gut. Then blood, intestines, stomach parts, oozing out."

Maybe I could see what she meant about not exactly fitting the first daughter's profile.

"See, this is another thing I'd have to give up," she said. She tossed the ball to me. "People don't play baseball when they're in the White House."

What was she talking about? "They don't?" I asked.

"Have you ever seen a baseball game in the Rose Garden?" she asked.

"Well, no. But it's a garden. With roses. Not that I know much about it—"

"Obviously. It's where they have press conferences," she said. "And egg rolls."

"Why would they have egg rolls?" I asked. "Is it a Chinese garden?"

"Because of Easter, you idiot. No, wait, the Easter egg roll event is on the lawn. Lawn, garden, whatever," she said, lightly tossing the ball back to me.

"If they have so much space, they might have private baseball diamonds you don't even know about," I said.

"They don't," she said. "I checked."

"When did you check?" Toss.

"We went there for a governors' reception two years ago," she said. Toss. "I hated it."

"Why? What happened?" I asked.

"The kids from the Eastern states were mean to me," she explained. "They put hot sauce in my punch."

I burst out laughing, and she glared at me. "Look at this as your revenge," I said. "They're not going to live there, are they? You have the once-in-a-lifetime chance to live at the White House. Do you know how much other kids would give to be in your place?"

She looked at me. "Do you enjoy being followed all over and quoted and yelled at all the time to smile for a picture?" she asked.

"Hm." I had to think about that for a minute. Come to think of it, this was the first time in a few days that I'd been outside without anyone recognizing me. It was really relaxing. Maybe Emma was right. I didn't think I could take being followed and quoted everywhere I went. Maybe she *wasn't* crazy not to want all the attention that came with being a successful politician's kid.

All of a sudden, I saw several of the missing pigs running along the side of the highway, toward us. A farmer was chasing them, calling out, "Soo-ee! Soo-ee!" and holding a bucket of slop.

They mostly ignored him and kept running, but a few pigs stopped to check out the bucket. A few other pigs stopped right behind Emma to do their business, as my dad calls it when we take Sassafras for a walk.

All I can say about what happened next is that I couldn't help myself.

"Look!" I cried. "That one looks just like Wilbur! Doesn't it?"

"Which one?" Emma asked.

"That one!" I pointed behind her.

She turned around to look, and, well, one good push deserves another, right? I pushed her, she lost her balance, and, waving her arms wildly, landed right in, uh, something that had been left by one of the pigs.

The look on her face was totally priceless. "Ewwwwwww!" she yelled.

If only I'd had a smartphone. That video would have been on YouTube instantly.

She jumped to her feet, gasping in horror. "Mom!

Hellllp!" Emma yelled at the top of her lungs. "Help meeeee!"

"Way to not draw attention to yourself," I said as the governor, her handlers, campaign workers, and a cluster of reporters and fans came running down the highway toward us.

Emma glowered in my direction. "You did this to me!"

I smiled, enjoying how uncomfortable she looked. "Well, I told you I'd get you back, didn't I? And if there's one thing you should know about me, it's that I never go back on my word."

"I hate you!" she screamed. "Mom!"

13

"I can't believe you made me take a shower at a rest area." Emma walked out of the ladies' lounge at a truck stop outside Goshen, Indiana, with a towel wrapped around her head.

"It's not a rest area. It's a truck stop," her mother corrected her.

Emma tossed her wet towel at her mother. "Whatever."

Governor Brandon caught the towel. "We have a very tight schedule today, so we don't have much choice. Is *that* what you're going to wear?" She stared at the torn jeans, faded Twins T-shirt, and old, well-worn Converse sneakers Emma was wearing. "Do you even have socks on?"

"Scandal, I know." Emma rolled her eyes.

The governor stepped back. "I didn't even know Kristen packed those ripped jeans."

"She didn't," said Emma. "I did. By the way, I threw out that flower dress," she said. "It was too disgusting. I didn't like that dress, anyway. Who even plays baseball in a dress? This isn't the nineteen seventies."

"Forties," her mother said.

"Whatever."

"Stop saying *whatever* all the time," her mother said. "And go pick out some new clothes to wear. We have appearances scheduled for the rest of the day."

"Fine. But first I'm going to get some gum." Emma started wandering through the candy aisles.

"Don't get bubble gum, and if you do, don't crack it! Where *is* Kristen, anyway?" Governor Brandon asked me, looking around.

"She was making some phone calls outside and told me to wait here," I said. "Stu and the general are over there." I pointed to the large-screen TV above the small food court. "Where else would they be? They might miss a poll result or something."

The governor put her hand to her mouth. "I just had a horrible thought. Don't tell me someone got a picture of Emma like that."

"Like what?" I asked. "In jeans?"

"No. *You* know. In pig poop," she said in a low tone, wrinkling her nose.

Something about hearing someone who might be president one day say the word *poop* just made me laugh. I couldn't stop laughing, actually.

"Oh, well," said the governor with a shrug.

"You can't control the news, only your reaction to it. Right, Aidan?" She walked beside me, closer to the food court. "I'm really glad we stopped here. While Emma was inside cleaning up, I visited with some truck drivers. It gave me a good chance to meet some hardworking men and women and listen to what they think isn't working in America. There's so much we need to do. And I feel like I'm formulating a plan that might get to the heart of the problem—"

"Governor, look at this. Absolutely insane," Stu said.

I looked at the TV. There was a photo of a golden retriever on a large screen behind a panel of guests sitting in a cable news studio at a semicircular desk. A large sign on the wall said THE REX MORGAN SHOW— YOUR TRUSTED SOURCE.

"So, what you're saying is that this dog has been misrepresented," said the show's host. I recognized him from a story about crazed killer bees hitting the Midwest, earlier in the summer.

For the record, we hadn't seen any killer bees in Fairmont. Ever.

"Yes, definitely," a woman agreed. Her name, printed on the screen, was Muffy Van Der Hooven, assistant vice president of the All-American Canine Club. "We can see in the face, the eyes, the way the fur descends from the belly. That is most definitely not a mutt."

Stu looked over at me. "You said your dog was a mutt."

I nodded. "She is."

"Nope. She's a purebred Labrador retriever," Stu said.

"She's a mutt. She's like four different breeds of dog," I said. "We got her from the pound when I was little."

"Wrong. Your parents got her from a puppy farm." Stu took off his glasses and rubbed his eyes. "Now PETA hates us and the ASPCA hates us. We probably already have people lined up to protest at our next appearance."

"We didn't buy her from a puppy farm! We adopted her from the pound," I said. "If the people there said she was a mutt, then that's what she is." All this talk about Sassafras made me miss her.

Back on TV, after a commercial break, the conversation was continuing. "Interesting, interesting. It makes a person wonder: What else has he said that isn't exactly true?" Rex asked. "A while back, Governor Brandon said she's relying on this boy to be her moral barometer for this campaign, her truth speaker—"

"You said that?" I asked.

The governor shook her head. "I never said that."

"If he would lie about a dog, what does that say about *her*?" Rex asked.

"Nothing. It says that *you're* a moron," the general said, glaring at the TV. "They should call this the *Rex Moron Show*."

On screen, Muffy cleared her throat. "That's not all. This dog is obviously overfed. I'd say we're talking about a case of animal neglect."

"How can you neglect someone by overfeeding them?" I wondered out loud. This person was making me feel very, very bad.

"Were this poor dog to somehow make it to my kennels, the first thing I would do is put her on a diet of love and good food," Muffy continued. "Then I'd seek to establish her lineage. Who knows? In a matter of months she might be showing at competitions, not languishing in small-town Ohio."

She said *Ohio* with her nose turned up, her mouth pursed, as if she were saying "So Bor-ing."

"She's not a horse. She's just our dog," I said. "A family dog. We love her. Who cares if she's a mutt or not?" I asked.

"Don't worry about this crackpot," said Stu, nodding at the screen. "He's got conspiracy theories for everything, even dog breeds. He'll attack us anywhere he can find a hole in our story."

"But it's not—I didn't have a hole," I said. "It's not like I was lying."

"Someone was," the general grumbled.

"They're the ones who are lying!" I said. "How

can they get away with that? They're just making up stuff out of thin air!"

"They're good. That's how." The general asked—more like ordered—the clerk behind the counter to change channels.

"Sassafras. Now the name, Sassafras," someone on another news station was asking. "What kind of significance does *that* have?"

He turned to someone named "James Hotchkins, dog name interpreter." "Well, the root of the sassafras tree was used at one time to make root beer and other drinks, but was found to cause cancer and liver damage. So it's a strange choice for a name. I'm not sure what we can infer, but perhaps Ivy would have been a better name. Ivy never killed anyone."

"No. That's right," agreed the host. "One would think that a small-town Ohio kid would name his dog something like Snickers or Rover."

"This is ridiculous!" I yelled. "Who cares what she's named? Anyway, it was my mom who named her."

"I've got an uneasy feeling," Stu said to the governor, behind me. "This might be the start of something very bad."

"I bet it's just a blip," said the governor, sounding confident. "They couldn't find anything bad about Aidan, so they decided to attack a defenseless animal."

"What was that?" asked Emma, walking over from the candy section. At the same time, Kristen was walking toward her, carrying a suitcase. "Who attacked an animal? Did the pigs die? Oh, please don't tell me any of the pigs died!"

"We haven't had a hog update," Kristen said. "Now, come on, let's get you dressed in something more appropriate."

"But what about the animals? What were you saying?" Emma asked, before Kristen could pull her away.

"It's not about the pigs. Wilbur didn't die," I told her. "Yet."

"Yet? What's that supposed to mean?" asked Emma.

"Well, where do you *think* they were going after the state fair?" I said. "To a pig farm to happily live out the rest of their lives?"

"Y-yes." Emma's eyes started to water, as if she was going to cry. "They're . . . they're not?" she asked.

"Come on, Emma. It's okay. Let's go fix your outfit." Kristen took her arm and gently pulled her away in the direction of the women's restroom.

"Listen, Aidan. I have to tell you something." The general rolled up his sleeves. "We've got a problem. Something's going on here. They are trying to drag you down."

"I'm just a kid," I said. "Why would it matter if they drag me down? I'm not running for president."

The general looked at me. "You are so naive. It's not cute anymore."

"What?" I asked a little nervously. I really didn't get it.

"The competition always tries to bring down the people close to a candidate," the general explained. "Once that happens, a candidacy is dead in the water."

They clicked to another channel. I recognized the reporter; he was one of the guys from a Cleveland station that always covered news in our area. I'd seen him at Christopher's football games. "We tried to find some friends of this so-called clarinet hero but were unable to locate any," he was saying. "Why? Apparently, he's not an easy person to be friends with."

My eyes widened as I saw the outside shots of my school, my house—and the FreezeStar Little League field. The camera zoomed in on my team, and on one teammate in particular.

"He's a disaster," said T.J. "A walking, talking disaster. He's the reason we lose our games. He can't hit."

They had interviewed T.J., of all people.

"They're going to take the word of T.J.?" I asked.

"Who's T.J.?" asked Stu.

"That jerk! Remember that really obnoxious kid who—" I stopped, listening to the interview.

"By the way, we're *glad* he's on the road," T.J. said. "Makes winning a whole lot easier. Now we have a shortstop who can actually hit," he went on.

"I can hit," I mumbled. Then I said it a little louder. "I can hit, you know."

"Who is this guy?" asked the general. "Kind of want to punch him in the gut."

"That's usually what he's doing to other kids," I said. "He's the stupidest, meanest—"

"Don't say *stupid*," the governor told me.

"Fine. He's not the sharpest knife in the drawer, then," I corrected myself. "But he is the biggest."

"They'll take anyone they can get on camera, bad-mouthing you. They're not interested in T.J.'s report card. Just yours," said the governor.

"But that's not fair," I said. "Plus, none of it is true."

The governor looked at me and raised an eyebrow.

"Well, okay, so I'm not the best hitter on the team. But I'm *improving*," I said. "Every year."

"I can't believe they're doing this to a kid. I mean, that's low. Really low," said Stu.

"That's because he was getting incredible results for us," said the general.

"Sassafras is a she," I said.

"Not the dog, Aidan. You," said the general. "They have to tear you down to get at us."

On each channel we turned to, the reporters

had gone around and interviewed everyone I'd ever known. My teachers, my dentist (who blamed my seven cavities on Lime Brains), Mrs. Saint Mane, the lady who lives down the block and always used to get mad at me for cutting across her lawn on my way to Simon's house.

Then I heard, "That's nothing compared to what we discovered when we spoke to his clarinet teacher. This self-proclaimed clarinet hero—"

"I never said I was a clarinet hero!" I cried. "That's what *they* said!"

"Take it easy, kid. It's going to be fine," said the general.

Here they were, in Mort's apartment, filming Mort. He'd say good things, I told myself. No matter how they tried to put words in his mouth, he'd tell them what I was really like. The reporter was listing all of Mort's qualifications and how many students he'd had over the years while Mort sipped his free McDonald's coffee.

"You've taught Aidan Schroeckenbauer. How does it make you feel when you hear people calling him the clarinet hero?"

"That's ridiculous. He didn't even like the clarinet at first," Mort said.

"Given the rocky start you had, would you say he then became a good student of music?" the reporter asked.

Mort shook his head. "No. He couldn't carry a tune in a paper bag. Also, he cheated on the duets."

"Did you really?" asked Stu.

"No!" *Mort, how could you?* I wanted to yell at the TV. That wasn't true. So why was he saying that?

T.J. insulting me was one thing, but Mort was another. Did he really think those things about me? Then why did he keep insisting I was his favorite pupil and telling me I had real talent? Was that all a lie just to keep my parents paying for lessons?

I felt like my entire town was ganging up on me. What did the world suddenly have against *me*? I was a nobody!

Everyone's smartphones started ringing. Stu and the general were answering multiple calls while other aides typed furiously on laptops. The governor was pacing and talking on the phone. Emergency meetings were being arranged: press conferences, interviews, and last-minute media blitzes.

I stood there, stunned. Just like that, the entire campaign was falling apart.

This definitely wasn't the way to run for president—not if you wanted to win.

14

I sank into a seat at the truck stop's food court, the soda machine on one side of me, Stu and the general at a table on the other. I was in a daze. Maybe if I splashed cold water in my face, I'd wake up from this bad dream.

A minute later, Emma sat down beside me, changed into campaigning clothes again: dressy black pants, a purple shirt, and black sandals. Her hair was styled, too. No wonder it had taken her so long.

She handed me a new box of Lime Brains. I didn't know whether I was more stunned by the fact she was being nice to me or by the fact that I was being dragged through the mud on a half-dozen news shows. Why did all these people care about me? And did anyone care that none of it was true? Where were the people who would stick up for me?

"Character assassination." The general shook his head. "If I've seen it once, I've seen it a thousand times. You know what they say. The bigger the target, the harder they fall."

"If he's a big target, I'd like to see a small one," Emma joked.

I frowned at her. "This isn't the time to be funny," I said. "Not that that was funny."

"Why not?" she said, cracking her gum.

"Because! Everyone back home just dragged my name through the mud!" I said.

"You've heard that politics can be rough," Stu said. "Well, it just got a lot rougher. Here, kid." Stu handed me his BlackBerry. "Make some calls, send some texts, do what you can. We're going on all-out damage control, and you should, too."

First I called my mom, but it went straight to her voice mail. Next I called Dad. Same thing. Why couldn't I reach anyone? I took a deep breath and called Mort. I had to know if that was how he really felt about me.

"All right, I've had just about enough of this," he said when he answered the phone. "If you can't leave me alone, I'll have the police—"

"Mort! Mort, it's me, Aidan," I said.

"Aidan!" he cried. "Oh, I'm so glad you called."

I wasn't sure I believed him, after what I'd heard him say. I wasn't sure I could even really talk to him, I was so hurt.

"I've been trying to get through to you, to your

parents," Mort said. "I can't get them, and I saw that interview—"

"You mean the one where you said I was a faker and couldn't even hold a clarinet?" I reminded him.

"No, no. What I said was that you were so little when you started coming to me for lessons that you could hardly hold the clarinet," Mort said. "That's different."

"Okay, but then how come you said I always cheated during the duets?" I asked.

"No, no, no . . . I did not say that!" Mort cried. "I said *other* pupils sometimes tried to get away with not playing along with me when we did duets, but you never did! I didn't say those things! Aidan, I wouldn't, I promise."

"But you did! I heard it with my own ears. The same ears that don't recognize pitch or notes or tunes or—"

"No! They edited everything. They took my words and edited them to make it sound bad. You've heard of splicing, right?" Mort asked. "When they showed up at my apartment, I knew they were shady. Why won't you believe me?"

"You—you said I couldn't carry a tune in a paper bag!" I reminded him.

"No, no. I said when we first started I used a paper bag to work on your breathing, to teach you proper technique and test your lung strength," Mort said. "Also, you might have hyperventilated one time. I made you blow into a paper bag."

"Oh."

"I've been calling that station in Cleveland all day to try to get them to retract the interview, but they won't listen to me. They won't take my calls," Mort complained. "They only want to talk to me if I have more dirt on you."

"*More* dirt?" I asked. "You didn't have any dirt, did you?"

"No, I didn't mean—look, Aidan. It's what I told you about politics. A shady business," Mort said.

"Yeah, I'm kind of figuring that out," I said. "Thanks for trying to clear things up. Keep trying, okay?"

"I'll walk to Cleveland if I have to," said Mort. "Fools. By the way, I caught you on *Wake Up, America!* Nice job, kid. And you know what? Anyone who actually talks to you for two seconds will know you're a good kid. Don't let them spin it."

But it was too late, I thought as we said goodbye and I gave the phone back to Stu. I was already getting spun. It reminded me of part of this awesome show *Vortex!*, where contestants get tossed into this spinning, turning wheel thing, and they have to climb their way out through foam. They keep slipping and sliding until the spin cycle slows down and they can leap out.

That was kind of what was going on here.

Except it wasn't stopping yet.

I stared at the TV. My stomach was starting to hurt. Maybe I was just hungry, I thought, so I popped open the box of Lime Brains Emma had given me.

I saw a reporter standing outside Fairstone Elementary, saying, "It was at this school that his socialist, big-government ideas took root."

"That's weird," said Emma. "I don't think you're that social."

"Some of his radical ideas were expressed in his most recent science project: converting corn husks to bicycle tires," the reporter said. "In this project, he claimed that, quote, 'Replacing as many cars as possible with bikes instead would solve America's energy crisis.' Not just lessen. Solve. This reporter has to ask: Why is Governor Brandon associating herself with radicals?"

"That's—that's not radical," Emma stammered. "That's true!"

"Everyone knows we need to end our dependence on foreign oil," said the governor. "Every candidate agrees on that! We just have different solutions for how to get it done."

The general leaned closer to me. "You're sure you don't want to get your hair cut?" he asked. "That could take care of a lot of this radical nonsense."

"My hair's not *that* long," I said.

"The Secret Service agents thought you were a girl," Emma said. "Remember?" She laughed.

"I was wearing a marching-band uniform. It has these girl spat things on the shoes, plus a furry helmet," I said.

Emma just stood there looking at me, smiling, arms crossed in front of her. "You don't look much like a girl—it's true. But you do have floppy hair. You have to admit. You're like a little California surfer dude stuck in Ohio."

"Just a little trim, not a military cut," said the general. "Although that could be arranged. Only take a couple minutes. Shave it right off."

"Would everyone stop using the word *little*? Please?" I said. As if being attacked on TV wasn't enough, now I was being mocked by the people who were supposed to be working with me?

"General, what are you talking about? Cut his hair? We can't change a thing about him!" said the governor.

The general looked at her as if she were suddenly speaking a foreign language. "Why on earth not?"

"That would be wrong. We can't go around changing people just because it suits the campaign."

Emma looked like she was about to burst. I could have sworn I saw steam coming out of her ears. "Really, Mom? Really?"

"Hold on a second." Stu pointed at the TV. "What's Rex Moron talking about now?"

"This is Rex Morgan, reporting live from the Fairstone town hall, where I've attempted to locate the birth record for one Aidan Schroeckenbauer, with no success. The town clerk insists that only blood relatives and legal guardians are allowed access to this information, but this reporter can't help but wonder: What is this town hiding about their clarinet hero, and why?" He leaned in to the camera and whispered dramatically, "Could it be that he is in fact much older than he claims, and therefore ineligible to play in Little League?"

"Have they ever *looked* at a picture of you?" asked Emma.

"No kidding. If he were older than he claims, wouldn't he be that much *taller*? Idiot!" Stu screamed at the television. "You're an idiot, sir!"

That was followed by a report questioning whether my parents paid their income taxes, and why my grandmother had had a knee replacement and whether the government had paid for it, and last, did I even have asthma, or was that just for show?

"What I've observed, certainly, on the campaign trail, is that he has no trouble whatsoever breathing," Rex Morgan went on. "I've never even seen him take out his inhaler. Now, we can't get to his medical records, because that, too, is privileged information, but—this suggests that Governor Brandon's top aides did not really check out this alleged twelve-year-old before they invited him to speak for the campaign. Is that the kind of judgment we want in the White House?"

Suddenly, everyone at the truck stop was staring at me as if I was a terrible, horrible person. As if I should be in jail.

"Turn it off," said the general with a sigh. "I hate Rex Moron."

"Actually, I think we'll keep watching it," the clerk behind the counter said to him in a not-all-that-friendly tone.

"The man is certifiable. You realize that," the general said with a frown.

"Oh, my goodness—look at the time, everybody!" said the governor. "We've got to move on down the road. I certainly enjoyed meeting with each of you." She tried to shake hands with a few people, but they edged away, looking uninterested. "You don't really *believe* all that stuff, do you?" she asked nervously. "Aidan's a good kid. This is just made-up stuff to try to hurt me. Obviously, my competitors have decided to step up their games and play dirty. I mean, is that how scared they are of change? That they attack a twelve-year-old?"

"You *are* twelve, right?" Stu whispered to me as we headed for the exit.

I didn't bother responding. I had a feeling I was living on borrowed time here. But I wasn't going down without a fight. As we made our way back onto the bus, I turned to confront Emma. "I think I know what's going on here."

"What?" She cracked her gum, right in my face.

"I can't believe you did this to me. Just because I pushed you into some pig poop," I said. "Are you really that determined to see your mom lose?"

"No. What are you talking about? And don't talk so loud," she whispered.

"All the attacks on my character. You're the one who made that happen," I said. "It was you, not the other campaigns, wasn't it? Not that you'd ever admit it, but—"

"Me? How would I have the power and connections to do that?" Emma asked.

"Please. You're the daughter of a popular presidential candidate," I reminded her. "You have all kinds of power."

"Me? Power?" she scoffed. "Have you noticed that I don't get to do anything I want?"

"If you wanted something to happen, you could do it. You've been living in the governor's mansion for the past few years," I pointed out. "You *know* people. And you told me you wanted me to bring down the campaign but that I was messing up.

You said you were going to take care of it yourself. You even threatened me, remember?"

"But I—I would never attack someone's family," Emma said. "I know what that feels like!"

"Then why did you do it?" I asked.

"I didn't!" she yelled.

"Yes, you did!" I pushed her a little. She shoved me back. We started pushing and shoving each other.

"Kids, kids!" Kristen yelled, pulling us apart. "Enough already! Get on the bus!"

I marched up the steps after Emma, with Kristen herding us as if we were a couple of out-of-control pigs.

A somber group of campaign workers sat in the front of the bus. They were slouched against windows, sort of dazed. By their expressions, you'd think they'd just found out the world was ending. Was the campaign in that much trouble? Because of me?

I sat toward the back, the way I always did. A few minutes after we headed out of the parking lot, Stu came to get me. I headed up front to the couch area, where the campaign staff did all its plotting.

The governor patted the seat next to her. Emma, never one to butt out, followed and stood behind me, in the aisle. Stu and the general were on the sofa facing us, looking very serious. "Aidan, listen," the governor said. "This is hard for me to say. I know it'll be hard for you to hear."

"You want me to leave, I know. And it's okay," I said. "No one wants out of here more than I do." I glared at Emma over my shoulder.

It would only take me a few years to fix my image. Five, tops. I braced myself. Now what? I tossed a couple of Lime Brains into my mouth.

"It's not that. Yet. It's just . . . you've been good to us, I think, so we want to be honest with you," the governor said. "Now, some evidence has been uncovered that indicates . . . well . . . listen. Sometimes in life we discover things that—"

"Spit it out already, Bettina," the general said. "Kid, your mother wasn't laid off because of the economy. She may have been fired. And you know why? Because she's allegedly been spying for the competition."

"Spying?" I repeated. "My *mom*?"

"A Chinese corporation," Stu said. "They're making a big splash in the American appliance market, making good stuff for low prices. It's called— well, I can't pronounce it in Chinese, but it translates to Cold Rainbow."

"C-C-Cold Rainbow?" I sputtered. I was in shock. Even my teeth were chattering. My mom—spying at FreezeStar? They couldn't be serious. Not my mom. She wouldn't do something like that.

All of a sudden I couldn't breathe.

"I know it must be a huge shock, but we felt we

had to tell you. We've been looking into the story, and it may not hold up. There are some inconsistencies and they're denying the whole thing, but it has the ring of truth." The governor gave me a sympathetic smile. "I'm so sorry," she said. "From what I know of you, your mom's a good person and a great mom, and if she was doing this, it was only to support her family. This recession has put people in a bind—"

"Excuse me, but are you going to sit here and tell me it's okay to give out trade secrets?" the general asked.

"Aidan? What do you have to say?" asked Stu. "Does this come as a total surprise? Do you think it has any root in reality, or did you see any signs—"

I shook my head. There were no signs because it wasn't true! I was gasping for air. I pointed at my throat. I needed help. I needed my inhaler! I wasn't getting any air!

"Oh, my gosh," Kristen said, fanning her face. "He's choking. Or he's having an asthma attack. He can't breathe!"

"I'll go find his inhaler," Emma said, dashing to the back of the bus. Seconds later she came back, holding something that was definitely not my inhaler. "I couldn't find it, but I got this!"

Then she jabbed a needle into my leg.

15

"Ow!" The shock of it made me cough out the Lime Brain that had gotten stuck in my windpipe. "Ow!" I screamed again. "What are you trying to do, kill me?"

"It worked, didn't it?" Emma replied smugly. "I held it there for ten seconds. That's right, isn't it, Mom?"

The governor leaped to her feet. "Emma, that's for allergic reactions! That's a prescription for you! You don't go around just jabbing people!"

"I was choking on a Lime Brain, not freaking out from peanut butter. Who doesn't know the international sign of choking?" I asked as I rubbed my thigh. I felt this surge of energy running all around my body as the medicine circulated.

"I know, but I thought you were choking because you were allergic to something," Emma said.

"I do know one thing. Once you administer

an EpiPen you have to be seen by a doctor. Immediately." Stu ran up to talk to the bus driver, while the governor had me lie down on the sofa. I didn't feel like lying down. I felt like running beside the bus. What if I was allergic to the antiallergic stuff?

Emma was hovering beside me, looking worried. "Is he going to be okay?" she asked. "I'm really sorry. I just—you weren't breathing right—I thought your throat was closing up—"

"Emma, give him some air. He's fine. He'll be fine." The governor tapped my ankle. "You're fine, right?"

I nodded. My throat felt sore, but I wasn't going to die on anyone.

"We'll be at the hospital soon. I'll sit here with you until we get there. Do you want me to call your parents, or would that just make them worry more?" she asked.

"Call them when we get there," I said. "Please."

"Not a problem. Oh, Aidan. You're not having a very good day, are you? And it's all my fault." The governor sighed.

"And mine," Emma said. "I'm sorry. I *guess* I overreacted."

I raised an eyebrow. "You guess?"

"I have a feeling we're not making it to the Elkhart County Fair," said the general. He picked up his phone. "Let me make some calls."

. . .

At the hospital in Goshen, Indiana, I was seen right away by an emergency-room doctor. I quickly explained the situation.

"What are you saying?" the doctor asked. "You choked on a piece of candy? It wasn't asthma at all? And you got the EpiPen in your leg?" She was trying not to laugh but she didn't succeed. "Some people," she said.

"Exactly," I said.

"Can I see the box of candy?" she asked.

I took the crumpled box out of the front pocket of my sweatshirt. Only a few pieces were left. I was ready to toss them. I was pretty sure I'd never eat Lime Brains again. I had this burning lime flavor in my throat that felt like it would never go away.

"You've eaten these before. Correct?" the doctor asked as she skimmed the list of ingredients.

I nodded. "A million times."

"Are these things actually any good? Green number forty-eight. I've never heard of that one. Of course, that doesn't mean you couldn't be allergic— people develop allergies at any time, at all ages, even to things they've been exposed to multiple times. But if you're saying you choked, then, basically, you aspirated a Lime Brain."

"What does that mean?" I asked.

"You inhaled one. I'm guessing more than one, actually. You might have a sore throat for the rest of the day, but you're perfectly clear to leave. Just sit here for a bit and relax, drink some water. I'll get the paperwork started for your discharge."

The TV at the end of the bed was on, with the volume turned down low. I was getting so sick of TV, I didn't care if we ever got cable again. If we did, I'd never watch it.

Headlines were scrolling across the bottom of the screen. CAMPAIGN DERAILED BY MEDICAL EMERGENCY . . . "CLARINET HERO" ON LIFE SUPPORT . . . CHINA'S COLD RAINBOW DENIES TALK OF CLARINET-HERO MOM . . . PULLING THE PLUG ON THE RAINBOW CAMPAIGN . . .

"I'm not dead!" I screamed at the TV.

"Glad to hear it." The general walked into the room. "I was worried about you, kid. You went pale. Real pale."

"Yeah, well. You were probably only worried because if I died, it would hurt the campaign," I said. "The poll numbers would drop."

"That's not true," he said. "I was genuinely concerned."

"About the poll numbers," I said.

The general frowned at me. "For your information, I don't think they can drop any farther than they already have. You know the term *free fall*?"

I didn't know what to say to him. I didn't care about the election anymore. All I cared about was the fact that everyone was attacking me and my family. And I still needed to get back at Emma for jabbing me with her EpiPen.

Suddenly, I saw a picture of my mom's face on TV. A reporter was standing on our front doorstep! My dad opened the door, said "No comment," and then slammed it shut again.

"No comment?" What was that supposed to mean? Shouldn't he tell them that there was no truth at all to the story, to any of the stories? That he was going to sue them if they kept talking about our family that way?

Then my brother opened the door. He flashed his school-picture smile. "Hi. Christopher Schroeckenbauer here. No comment, but I can tell you that none of this is true. Tell Aidan I said hi." He smiled again, then quickly closed the door.

I smiled and thought about how I'd kind of missed Christopher, even if he did have to be in the spotlight at all times. He might be the right person for his job, but I wasn't—not anymore.

"My mom's not a spy," I said to the general.

"How do you know?" asked the general. "The children are always the last to know."

I glared at him. "I just know—that's all!" I fiddled with my hospital ID bracelet. "My mom would never do that. She isn't that person," I said. "I can't believe you're taking some reporter's word over mine!"

"I'm not. These are just allegations," said the general. "Innocent until proven guilty. That's the American system."

"She's not guilty! This is all totally made up!" I cried.

I focused on the TV again. They were running a story about how FreezeStar was a questionable company. How the town itself was struggling to get by. I thought about Simon saying he wanted to whack that reporter for criticizing our town. I kind of felt the same way now. This attack on me and my family was like a snowball, rolling down a hill, getting bigger and bigger. I had to stop it before it crushed everyone in its path.

That's when I knew what I needed to do.

"Your paperwork is all done. You've been discharged and you're free to go," said the doctor. I'd been so busy thinking and worrying that I hadn't even seen her come in.

She said I had nothing to worry about, that everything checked out. Then she came to the waiting room with me, and she and Emma had a short discussion about the proper use of EpiPens. "Oh, and please tell the governor I'm voting for her!" she called as we headed for the exit with the general.

"Great, one more vote," Emma muttered as we walked behind him.

"Is that all you can say?" I asked.

She looked at me as if I'd lost my mind. "What do you want me to say?"

"I don't know. How about sorry? Sorry I stuck your leg with a sharp needle and caused you tons of pain and a racing heartbeat?" I said.

"Look, I already said I was sorry," Emma reminded me. "How many times do you expect me to say it?"

"I don't know. How about until my leg stops hurting?" I sighed. "You know what? Never mind. I'm not going to be around much longer."

"Why?" she asked. "Where are you going?" She trotted after me toward the exit.

The governor was standing outside, campaigning as always, shaking hands, which didn't seem like a good idea considering some people were heading into the emergency room and probably had the flu or something worse. She wasn't even flinching. She really loved people. Even sick and injured ones.

"Aidan," Emma said, still tagging after me. "What do you mean, you won't be around much longer?"

I didn't answer her, because as soon as we walked out of the hospital, the media swarmed around us.

"What happened, Aidan?" a reporter from CNN asked.

"Are you okay?" asked an NBC reporter.

A Fox News reporter leaned in close to me. "What do you have to say about your mother allegedly being a corporate spy?"

I blinked at the camera flashes. Even though I didn't want to have sympathy for Emma, I was starting to understand how this would make her feel, day after day.

"Are you happy with yourselves now?" the governor asked as a dozen reporters surrounded me with their microphones. "You've taken a young boy and frightened him half to death with your made-up stories."

"That's okay, Governor. I want them near me right now. I have a statement to make," I said. "I'm going home."

"You can't leave mid-campaign!" Stu called after me as I walked over to the bus. "You can't leave right now! We have to clear your name. If we don't clear *your* name, we can't clear the governor's name."

"Well, I can't clear my name without going back home," I said. "Besides, am I really doing anything to help you guys at this point?"

"Yes, of course you are. Come on, we'll go with you. We'll all go back to Fairstone and clear the air," said Stu, following me up the bus steps.

"We can't," said the general, who was right behind him. "We already had to pass on the county fair. Now we have got to make up time and hit Kalamazoo and Battle Creek—"

"Michigan?" I said. "We're going to Michigan now?"

"Yes, didn't we tell you?" Stu said. "We have a dozen events lined up tonight and tomorrow in the Detroit area—they're too important to miss!"

"No." I shook my head. "Just cancel."

"We can't cancel them, Aidan. These are fund-raisers. We need funds," said Stu. "Or there won't be a campaign to save."

I sat down in my seat and looked out the window, wondering how I could make this happen. Detroit was only a couple of hours by car from Fairstone, but it was definitely too far to walk.

"Let's make a deal, Aidan." The general tapped his fingers together. "Stick with us for two more days. We'll do these fund-raisers. We'll head back to Fairstone, right where this Midwestern tour got its first big push. You'll be done."

"Why does he get to be done?" asked Emma, slumping into the aisle seat right beside me. "When do I get to be done?"

The general ignored her question. "Listen, Aidan. We're going to talk this over. We'll work it out. Just give us a few minutes."

I didn't want to wait, but I needed time to come up with a plan. One, how was I going to get there on my own? Two, what would I do once I got there?

The grown-ups all sat in their conference area up front, and Emma leaned over to me. "What are you going to do if you leave?" she asked in a soft voice.

"Why do you care?" I asked.

"Because! Part of this is my fault," she said.

"No kidding. And now I have to fix everything,"

I said. "People think my mom's a spy; they think my clarinet playing is horrible and that I'm too old for Little League."

I was expecting her to make a crack about my height or my clarinet playing, but she didn't. "What are you going to do?" she asked.

"I don't know yet," I said. "But whatever it takes, I'll do it."

"Okay." Emma nodded. "Well, I'll help you."

"I don't want your help," I said. "You're the one who made all this happen in the first place! First you made me look like an idiot by pushing me across that stage. Then you switched out my clarinet music for a room-service menu. You told everyone a bunch of lies about me, then you tried to kill me with your EpiPen."

"It sounds bad when you say it like that," she said.

"And now there's this rumor about my mom! I mean, how do I know that didn't come from you?" I asked.

"Because it didn't. You have to believe me," she said.

"You're not that believable," I said. "Your track record is not very good. And all because you don't want to live in the White House!" I said. "Why don't you just tell your mother the truth?"

"The thing is that all these attacks on you, to try

to get to my mom and ruin her life, it's made me realize something," Emma said. "It's one thing if I don't want her elected. But it's totally different if other people get in the way of her dream. So I'm going to help her become president and not get in her way anymore."

"Seriously?" I asked.

She nodded.

"But why do you want to help me?" I asked.

"Because I've been where you are," she said. "Lots of times. And no kid wants to see her mom dragged through the mud. I know what that feels like. I'd never do that to you or wish that on anybody else."

Something about her voice made me think she was being honest for a change. "So, what do we do?" I asked.

"Well, I know what my mom would do. She'd make a five-point plan," said Emma. She reached into her backpack and pulled out a small notebook and a pen. "First things first. We start with an easy thing. You go on camera and say that you're twelve and hold up a copy of your birth certificate."

"I don't have one," I said.

"Your parents will," she said. "Once we get to Fairstone, this will all be easy."

"How are we going to get to Fairstone—without the rest of them?" I asked.

"It's just like when we were playing baseball. You totally underestimate me." She continued making notes on her list.

1. Birth cert.

2. E. interviews T.J.

"Your friend can help us, right?"

"What friend?" I asked.

"The one who came to say good-bye, gave you that awful candy," Emma said.

"Simon?"

"Yeah. Him." She nodded. "When we get a second of privacy, can you call him? Okay, good." She started writing again.

3. Get Simon to help. Not sure how yet.

4. Factory serenade.

5. On-camera interview with company rep.

"Kids?"

Emma and I nearly bonked heads as we both looked up to see Kristen standing over us. She was like our own personal rain cloud. "What's going on?" she asked.

"Oh." Emma quickly covered the notebook with her arm. "Nothing, really."

"Just doing some, you know. Hangman." I pretended I had a noose around my neck and did an imaginary jerk on the imaginary rope. It wasn't that far off from the truth of how I felt.

"He lost badly," said Emma. "What's going on up there?" She pointed to the front of the bus.

"Lots of strategy stuff. We need to get this train back on the track," said Kristen.

"Well, you're good at that," said Emma. "What's our next stop, since we had to skip the fair?"

Kristen consulted her BlackBerry. "I'm not sure about this, because things are constantly changing. Looks like we might have something in Kalamazoo? Anyway, that's not the big push. The big one is our visit to an auto plant near Detroit."

Emma nodded. "Sounds like a plan. Do you happen to know which one we're going to?"

"I'm not sure, but I can go check," said Kristen.

"Would you, please?" Emma asked.

"Sure. And I love those good manners," Kristen said. "Be right back."

"That's where we'll take off," Emma whispered to me after Kristen left us. "Just be ready when I tell you to run."

The auto plant wasn't the next stop. I stayed with
the campaign through a school visit in Kalamazoo
and a rally in Battle Creek outside a cereal company,
but I kept a low profile just in case people believed
what they were reading about me. I told the general
I thought it'd be best if I stayed on the bus, and he
didn't argue with me. Emma stayed on the bus,
too, making calls and planning, and I gazed out the
window at the big crowds, trying not to get upset
about the fact I'd be going home soon—going home a
total failure, that is.

Now I had finally gotten off the bus at the
assembly plant, and I was waiting for Emma to tell
me what to do. Governor Brandon was speaking in
front of a huge crowd of autoworkers who held up
union signs. They were chanting and pumping their
fists. Most of them seemed to support her, but a few
were heckling her, too.

Two men standing beside me were talking. "I

don't know a thing about her," the first one said, "but she seems to know what she's talking about."

"Me neither, but I'm impressed so far," the other guy said.

A woman leaned over. "Did you hear how she saved the Ford plant in Saint Paul?" she asked.

"Nah. Really?"

"Oh, yeah. She went to the mat for those guys," the woman said, and they all nodded, like this was a secret handshake test Governor Brandon had just passed.

"I'm not anti-union!" the governor was saying. "I'm pro-union! In fact, if it were up to me, everyone would have a union to represent their best interests. And you know who I'd start with? The working moms like the ones I've met here today," she said.

Women in the crowd went wild.

"And then the working dads! Behind every good American car, there's a team of workers making it into the best quality on the road today. They might be moms, dads, aunts, uncles, grandparents, but they all deserve decent wages and health care for their families! Everyone needs to have a voice. Everyone needs to be heard, and I'm the only one out here running for president who's listening!"

When a few people recognized me, they gave me high fives. I held back. I couldn't help wondering whether everyone actually believed all those crazy stories about me. Maybe they'd been busy at work and hadn't heard the stories yet. Or maybe they had heard them but they were cutting me some slack.

Then again, some of them might believe my mom was spying for a Chinese company. So maybe not.

Emma pulled on my arm, holding me back from the wave of supporters heading for the makeshift stage in the parking lot to shake the governor's hand or exchange a few words with her. I was being swept along with the tide, but Emma strong-armed me to the side. "We're out of here," she said.

"What about Kristen?" I asked. "Won't she notice?" I looked around. "Where is she, anyway?"

"I sent her on an errand to get me a specific kind of kiwi-mango-strawberry juice that's really hard to find," Emma said.

"Sounds disgusting," I said, making a face.

Emma snapped my arm with her finger. "It's not real, you idiot. I made it up to keep her away from us. She won't be back for fifteen minutes, at least."

"Kiwi juice? That's your alibi? Okay," I grunted as I tried to squeeze past two very tall, very strong men. "What about the Secret Service?" It seemed as if their ranks had increased lately, and I didn't recognize half of the new agents. That might be good. They might not know me, either. But Emma? They'd never let her out of their sight.

"Too busy making sure Mom gets through the

crowd safely. They're worried about this one. Twice as many people showed up as they were expecting, and it's dicey," Emma said.

"Yeah, but isn't that more reason for them to watch you carefully?" I argued.

"They think they're so smart with their code names. Ponytail. I mean, who is that fooling? No, we can get away. Watch this. Come on," Emma said, leading me away from the chaos.

"Where are we going?" I asked. We hadn't had time to go over our plan because Stu and the general had spent the last twenty minutes before we arrived reviewing Operation Image Repair with me. Emma and I hadn't had a second of time to talk in private. "Where's my stuff?" I asked Emma.

"I already dropped it where it needs to be. Just come on!" she urged. We made it toward the exit, and she suddenly stopped beside an extremely large beige SUV that kind of looked like a tank. It had big tires that were almost as tall as me.

"Well?" she said. "What are you waiting for? Get in."

How? I was wondering. "What is this?" I asked.

"It's called a Road Stormer. Latest thing out of Detroit," she said. "I think they make it here. I don't know, I asked for something really secure. They said it has some kind of armor in the doors." She shrugged. "Sounded good enough to me."

"Is this for us?" I asked. "How did you ...?"

"You said I had a lot of power. Well, I'm using it." She climbed up into the SUV, using a little ladder that unfolded when the door was opened. I followed her. She talked to the driver for a minute, then sat down next to me. "I called a private car service, told them we're making a round trip so I can drop you off. I have access to my mom's credit cards, you know, in case of emergency."

"But everyone's going to panic when they realize we're gone," I said, shifting to get comfortable in the giant backseat. I felt like I was getting onto an amusement park ride and a bar should drop down to protect me. "These cars are terrible for the environment," I said, fastening my seat belt.

"Yeah, but they're really cool," Emma said. "Besides, this one uses ethanol. What, you want to show up back home in an old pickup or something? Okay, so I'll text Mom in a minute. She won't have time to read the text until the event's over, but when she reads it, she'll know we're okay," Emma said confidently. "Don't worry, I've got it all figured it out." She smiled. "They won't report us as missing, because it'll look bad for them. They'll just pretend we're on the bus until we all meet up again, and they can prove it. Anyway, I'll call her once we're in Fairstone. We can even send a picture of us with your mom if she needs more proof. They'll finish tonight's fund-raiser, then someone will come to haul me back. That gives us tonight to get this done."

"How do we get everything on our list all done tonight?" I asked.

"We work fast. Just like everyone else in TV news." Emma took out her phone. "I'm going to call some news stations."

When we breezed through the Fairstone exit two hours later, I'd never been so glad to see a trollbooth in my life. We cruised through town, which looked really strange, as if I'd been away for months, not days, as if I was seeing it for the first time.

A white van was parked at the curb outside my house when we pulled up in front. I saw the initials of a Toledo TV station on the side. Other than them, there was an eerie quiet in the neighborhood. It felt like a ghost town.

We said hi to the reporter and the camera operator covering the story and walked up to the front door. I couldn't wait to see everyone. I didn't hear Sassafras barking, which was strange. We rang the doorbell. Nobody answered at first.

"Mom!" I called out, knocking on the door. "Mom, it's me, Aidan!"

I saw the curtains in the living room move a little. Seconds later, Mom threw open the door. "Aidan!"

she shrieked, and threw her arms around me. "What are you . . . ? Who . . . ?"

I hugged her tight. As much as I'd been through, she'd had it even worse. "This is my friend Emma," I said. "The governor's daughter. She's here to help me clear up a few things about our family. And me."

"Hi!" Emma waved. "I really hate it when people attack my mom, too."

"What about *them*?" Mom turned up her nose at the reporter and cameraman standing behind me.

"We're looking to help you retell your small-town story," said the reporter. "We feel as though maybe the national media got it wrong over the past couple of days. Sure, it's good for the ratings, but is any of it true?"

My mom shook her head. "Nope."

"When you look bad, we look bad," said the reporter. "So, let's repair your image."

"I like you," said my mom, smiling a little.

"Where is everyone?" I asked, glancing past her. She was keeping the door closed behind her as if a tornado were trying to get inside.

"Christopher is out with friends. Dad's working a double shift, and—well, Sassafras is hiding at your grandparents' house, in the country." She lowered her voice. "Dog-napping threats have been made."

Great. My dog had joined the witness protection program. "First things first, Mom. Do you have my birth certificate? I have to prove I'm as old as I say I am."

"Ridiculous. I'll just tell them," Mom said. "Again."

"Well, no offense, but you're not totally reliable right now," Emma reminded her.

"Yeah, Mom. You have to come up with the actual piece of paper, and these nice guys will film it," I said.

"But don't worry, Mrs. Schroeckenbauer," said Emma. "We're going to set everything straight."

I was shocked. Not only was she being nice, but she pronounced my last name right.

"Come on in, everyone, and have something to eat," Mom said, "while I find that birth certificate."

"This is really your house?" Emma asked when she walked in and started looking around.

"Yeah . . ." I said slowly. I waited for her insults.

"It's nice," she said. "It makes me miss home."

Our next stop was FreezeStar Field. The news van was right behind us, and Emma was busy making calls to various people, making sure our story was picked up by other stations. "Share the video of the birth certificate. Let everyone know he's only twelve," she said. "He's not a liar."

"Thanks," I said as we climbed out of the Stormer.

"Don't thank me yet," she said, heading down

the embankment to the field. A game had just ended, and the scoreboard said, HOME: 3, AWAY: 10. All my teammates were lined up to shake hands on the third-base line. T.J. was at the end of the line. He hated to lose at anything. My uncle Robert was nudging him forward.

"Perfect. I can swoop right in for a gonzo interview," said Emma. "Mind if I borrow the mike on this one?" she asked the reporter.

"No problem," he said as she snatched it from his hands. "I guess."

Emma motioned for the cameraman to follow her and hurried over to T.J. "Surprise!" she said.

He looked at her, completely confused, and then at the camera, and then at me, and he smiled. "Shrieking, I knew you couldn't make it in Washington. I knew you were going to blow it."

"I wasn't *in* Washington," I said. "Obviously."

"And he didn't do anything wrong," Emma said.

"Aidan?" Uncle Robert asked. "Hey, bud!" He jabbed my shoulder with his fist. "I didn't know you were back!"

"Hey," I said, punching his shoulder right back. I waved at Simon, who was jogging in from left field. "Shh, we're filming here, okay?"

Emma turned to the camera with a big, friendly smile. "This is Emma Brandon, with the Brandon for President campaign. We're back in Fairstone, Ohio, trying to clear up a couple of issues. We're giving people a chance to set the record straight. With me is T.J. . . . . Somebody or other. That part's not important."

"Lewis," T.J. said. He wiped sweat from his forehead with the hem of his baseball shirt. Even though dusk was falling, it was a very hot night. "T.J. Lewis. My dad's the mayor."

"Okay, then you probably know how important it is to tell the truth," Emma said. "'Cause if you lie, it might make voters think that your *dad* lies." She waited for the words to sink in. "Now. We all saw an interview you did for *Entertainment Nightly: Political Edition*. You said the team was winning, with Aidan the Clarinet Hero gone. But isn't it true that you've actually *lost* two games since Aidan left?"

The camera panned to the scoreboard and then back to T.J.

"Well, uh—" he stammered. "I guess."

"And isn't it true that Aidan had the best stats on the team for fielding last year and is one of the best shortstops in the history of the FreezeStar Little League team?" she asked.

"Sure. Uh." T.J. took off his ball cap and rubbed his head.

"Have *you* ever won the batting title?" Emma asked him.

Simon was standing next to me by then, and he leaned over. "She's good," he said.

"No, I have—haven't, but—" T.J. stammered. "I probably will this summer. For the summer league."

"Really? Because about that," Emma said. "There are rumors that you may be using a juiced bat. Some people are saying that there's no way you can hit as far as you do with a normal bat. What do you say to that?"

"Uh, hold on a second. That's not true," said T.J.

I couldn't believe she was accusing him of cheating at baseball. Wasn't that going a little too far?

"It may be true," Emma said. "As far as we know. And there you have it, ladies and gentlemen. The view from the bench." She smiled, then turned off the mike. "And that's a wrap."

"A wrap? You didn't give me a chance to say anything!" T.J. whined.

"Exactly. Now you understand how this works," said Emma. She handed the mike to the reporter, then turned to me and Simon. "You guys ready for phase four?"

"Of course," said Simon. The three of us headed up to the giant SUV, where the driver was waiting for us. "All we have to do is go past my house and pick up my drums."

"Nice interview of T.J.," I said to Emma after we

climbed in and were headed down the road, with Simon giving directions to the driver. "How did you get to be such a good reporter?"

"Please. What did we watch all those news shows with the general for? We know how to do this," said Emma.

It was almost nine when we finally arrived at the FreezeStar factory: me, Emma, Simon and his drums, Christopher, and my mom. Fireflies were lighting up the dark spaces between streetlights.

The plant was massive. It was the length of a dozen football fields and about as wide. It looked sort of like a gray fortress, and we looked like little ants standing outside the chain-link fence surrounding the building.

I got out my clarinet, and Simon adjusted the snare drum around his neck. "Christopher, keep texting so we can get a crowd here," I said. He nodded, slouched in the backseat. "And Mom, stay put in the car and stay safe until we come get you."

"Okay, if you say so, but if I see any trouble, I will be out of here in a second to save you," she said.

"Mom, it's going to be fine," I assured her, closing the door.

"What do we do now?" Simon asked. "March or something?"

We both looked for Emma, to find out the game

plan. She walked around from the other side of the SUV, holding a flute.

"Where did you . . . ?" I asked.

"You never saw it, but I do travel with my flute."

"Okay, but I don't know any trios," I said.

"Yeah, me neither," she said. "But I figured there's strength in numbers."

We started with what we all knew from memory: the theme from *The Simpsons*.

So there we were: me wearing my baseball cap, playing the clarinet outside the company gates. Simon, still in his FreezeStar baseball uniform, playing drums, marching beside me. And Emma, the candidate's daughter, who'd insisted on dressing nicely because it would make her less suspicious, in front of the FreezeStar plant.

"If there was ever a photo op, this is it," the reporter said. He had the cameraman take several shots of us, playing as we marched on the sidewalk and standing on a bus bench to make our sound travel farther.

"My dad's inside. I wonder if he can hear me," I said.

I thought of my dad telling my mom, "You don't stand here and criticize the company, not here." What if what I was doing jeopardized my dad's job, got him in trouble? My mom was already out of work. I couldn't add my dad to the list. But I had to stand up for my mom, too. There was no way she was going to take the fall for FreezeStar. If there was a spy, which I doubted, she wasn't it.

"No one's going to hear us," said Simon.

"Yeah, but that's what the TV station is for." Emma coughed, clearing her throat. She turned to the camera as a security guard approached us.

"What exactly is going on here?" asked the guard. "May I help you?"

"Yes, please." Emma smiled. "We have a list of demands. And we will stand out here and play until management comes down."

The guard frowned. "There's nobody here right now who can help you with your . . . problem. Whatever it is."

"Come on, that can't be true," said Emma. "Can't someone come out and talk to us?"

He looked at me. "Don't I know you? Steve Schroeckenbauer's kid?"

"Yes, yes," I said enthusiastically. "It's me, Aidan!"

I expected him to be nicer after that, but no. "What do you want?" The guard narrowed his eyes at Emma.

"The truth—that's all," I said.

"We're following up on the untrue rumor about Aidan's mother giving trade secrets to Cold Rainbow," said Emma. "We know it's not true. We need someone from FreezeStar to come out here and refute it on camera."

"Well, why don't you write a letter?" The guard looked at the cameras. "No cameras allowed on company property. Industry secrets to protect."

"We're on the public sidewalk," said the reporter. "Same as these kids."

"But you can't do this!" the guard cried as Simon began to play the drum again. "There's a noise ordinance."

"Please, you think that's loud? You should hear your trucks," I said.

"But there's a senior residence in the area—"

"Exactly. This will keep them awake all night. Which is why you should get someone down here ASAP to talk to us. I'm sure we can clear this up," Emma said with a sweet smile. "Please. We don't want trouble. We totally respect your authority here." She looked—and sounded—a lot like her mother.

"Well, okay, I'll ask," the guard finally said.

"He'd never make it in the Secret Service," Emma said to me once he was standing off to the side, making a call.

Simon, Emma, and I kept playing and marching, back and forth while we waited for someone to come talk to us. Just as I was feeling like it was almost time to give up, there was Mort, holding his clarinet.

"Got room for one more?" he asked.

"Hey! You heard us!" I said.

"Who wouldn't? Wait, I take that back. The other blue-hairs are all asleep by now," he complained. "Anyway, what's-her-name called me, left a message." He pointed at Emma. "What's the plan?"

"Play until they agree to talk to us and clear my mom's name," I said.

"Thought that was it." Mort nodded. "Old-school protest. Count me in."

We kept playing, and as the minutes wore on, people started to show up. Christopher was doing a good job calling and texting everyone he knew, and they were bringing their families. The crowd continued to grow as Mort, Emma, Simon, and I played "When the Saints Go Marching In."

Soon, a fancy-looking car pulled up and was buzzed through the gates. A short time later, a woman in a suit came out to talk to us. As she got closer, I saw that she wore the FreezeStar employee ID tag around her neck, the same one my dad had.

I ran over to the SUV to get Mom. We hurried back to Emma and the news crew, just in time to hear the woman introduce herself on camera. "Hello. My name is Mary Afton, and I'm senior vice president and director of human resources at FreezeStar. I'm here tonight to address some questions that have been brought to my attention," she said with a smile.

"Hello, Mary," my mom said, stepping forward.

"Oh, Tricia, it's you," said Mary. "How are you?"

One of the reporters suggested it might be a good idea to climb higher than the crowd, so they could be seen and heard by everyone. Mom and Ms. Afton stood on the bus bench, while Emma, Simon, and I climbed onto the roof of the SUV for a better view.

"We're here because we'd really like to—no, we need to—clear up some misunderstandings," my mom said. "There's this crazy story in the news about me, about how I got fired because I was a spy. First of all, I'm not a spy. Second of all, I'm on temporary leave—not fired. Right?"

Ms. Afton nodded. "Yes, that's right. Who's saying that you're a spy? That's ridiculous." She laughed.

"The press is ridiculous," said my mom. She glanced down at the cameraman. "No offense. I like you guys. Could someone from FreezeStar please tell the world that I'm no corporate spy?"

"Whoever is listening, that story is absurd," said Ms. Afton. "Tricia Schroeckenbauer is not a spy."

"Okay," said Emma, sliding down from the SUV and stepping forward, as the camera swiveled in her direction. "But this is about getting the truth out there, because it affects me and my mom as a candidate. *Why* did you have to lay off Mrs. Schroeckenbauer?"

"Our factory orders rise and fall, depending on

214

the economy. We often have to adjust our employee numbers," Ms. Afton said.

"And is that what happened? Not enough people buying freezers?" Emma asked, looking up at Ms. Afton.

"That's absolutely correct. I can tell you that Mrs. Schroeckenbauer is no spy," Ms. Afton repeated.

Mom pumped her first in the air. "Yes! Thank you!"

"Has she done anything wrong to justify her being among the first group of layoffs?" a reporter called from the front row of the crowd.

"The first group?" Ms. Afton shook her head. "She was in the third group, according to my records. Because of her long record of loyalty and hard work, she was among the last to be furloughed. And as soon as we can hire her back, we will."

While I was perched on the SUV, I saw a figure in the darkness, pushing his way from the back of the crowd to the front. He was headed straight for us. No, wait. He was heading right for Emma, carrying something that looked like it might be a stick in his right hand. Was it a stick? Why would he— Wait. Maybe it was a rifle! My heart started to pound.

I slid off the top of the SUV, wondering how I could intercept him—or her. This was all my fault! I was panicking. This was why Emma shouldn't travel without her Secret Service agents. This was why she needed security.

If anything happened to her while she was trying to help me, I'd never forgive myself.

Or wait—maybe the person was headed for my mom. Maybe he thought *she* was the real traitor. Or maybe he was the real spy.

There was no time to lose. I slipped into the crowd and crept up behind him. He was taller than me, with broad shoulders, and moved briskly. He looked like he might play football. He was definitely carrying a stick, and he clearly meant trouble.

"Excuse me," I said, but my voice came out sounding shaky and weak. "Hey!" I yelled. "Hey, you! Stop!" I called.

He began to turn around, and I gripped my clarinet, bell in front, as if it were my favorite bat. Then I took a swing for the fences—right at his gut!

18

He doubled over, gasping in pain, clutching his stomach.

It was T.J.

That Jerk!

He dropped the aluminum bat he'd been holding, and it clanged against the concrete sidewalk. It rolled away from him, into the gutter.

"You?" I panted, suddenly out of breath. "What are you doing?"

"I . . . should . . . ask . . . you," he gasped. Then he got his wind back and tried to shove me away.

I stumbled a little but managed to keep my balance. "You were headed straight for Emma. I thought you were going to attack her," I said.

"Well, I was," T.J. admitted. "I want her to take back what she said about me."

"By attacking her with a baseball bat? You really think that would work?" I asked.

"I was just going to show her the bat, not attack

her! It's not a juiced bat!" he cried. "It's my lucky bat—that's all."

A smaller crowd within the big crowd began gathering around us. I saw kids from school pressing in to get a better view.

"You can't stop me," T.J. said, trying to push past me, but I barred his way with my clarinet, forcing it against his waist like a gate.

"*Move*, Shrieking," he said, picking up the bat.

"You're not going up there," I said. "You're not going to do anything. Leave her alone!"

"Oh, so suddenly you're best friends?" T.J. scoffed. He drove his body into mine like a fullback.

I leaned back at him, trying to think of some Secret Service moves I could use. Why had I never gotten some tips from them?

"I'm sick of you being on TV," T.J. said, pushing me again. "I'm tired of seeing your face!"

"Jealous much?" I asked, pushing back. I was vaguely aware of the crowd around us getting bigger.

"I'm not jealous. You're annoying is all. And the stuff you say isn't even true." He grunted as he struggled to push me aside. "I've never used a juiced bat. Never."

"Then maybe now you know how it feels when people lie about you on the news!" I yelled, wincing from the hold he now had on my arms. I was about to drop my clarinet.

"Out of my way, Shrieking!" He gave one last shove and hurled me to the ground. I landed nose-first, and my clarinet clattered onto the pavement beside me. I reached out and grabbed his ankles as he went past me, and he dropped with an awkward thud.

"Nice takedown!" a kid yelled.

"Fight!" somebody else yelled, and the crowd around us grew even bigger, so that I could feel it looming over me.

T.J. and I wrestled on the sidewalk. Before he could pin me, I wriggled out from underneath him and jumped to my feet. T.J. got up and swung a punch at my face, but I ducked just in time—just as the general caught T.J.'s fist in midair. Then he lifted up T.J. by his belt loops. "Is there a problem here?" he asked in a deep voice.

I did a double take. When did the general show up?

"Put me down!" T.J. cried.

My face was killing me, and I thought I might have a bloody nose. Still, I smiled when I saw T.J. being dangled in the air by the general. Maybe the general was a little gruff and obsessed with politics, but he was a pretty cool guy all the same.

"Young man, I'd advise you to verbalize your opinions in the future," the general said as he shifted T.J. to a more neutral position—sideways. "Words speak louder than fists."

"Put me down!" T.J. cried again. "I'm going to sue you!"

Emma glowered at T.J., her fists raised. "You think you can just punch people for no reason?" she asked him.

Most of the cameras were now trailing Governor Brandon, who was walking briskly from the Fresh Idea Party bus through the crowd. Microphones zoomed in from all directions like a swarm of mosquitoes.

"Emma!" cried the governor. "Oh, my goodness, I'm so glad to see you're all right. But could you please stop fighting?"

Emma's hands dropped to her sides.

"And, uh, you, too, General?" the governor said.

The general gently set T.J. back down, and I took a few steps back, wary of what T.J. might do next.

Governor Brandon gave Emma a big hug, and at the same time, seemed to pull her a bit farther away from me and T.J. "What's going on here, Aidan?" she asked quietly. "Can't we all just get along?"

"Emma, would you care to comment?" asked a reporter.

"Nothing's going on. It was just a little dis-agreement—that's all," Emma said.

The reporter turned to me. "Aidan? Is that true?"

"Why would she lie? Nothing's going on. Nothing at all," I said. "Well, T.J. here was upset because we may have suggested he used a juiced bat. But he doesn't. We were wrong."

"And T.J.? Don't you have something to say?" asked Emma. "Like admit what you were wrong in saying?"

"Oh. Well, Aidan isn't a horrible player," T.J. said. "He's actually a pretty good shortstop sometimes. He's not why we lose games."

I shrugged. It wasn't much, but I'd take it. Fair enough.

T.J. picked up my clarinet and handed it to me. I handed him his bat. "Truce," he said. Then he walked away.

Mort walked up then and took my clarinet away from me. "I think you might have smashed a key or two. Or more. I'll take it home and see what I can do. If I can't repair it, I'll let you use one of mine until you get it fixed. See you Tuesday? Regular time?" he asked me.

"Regular time," I said, smiling.

The crowd broke up a few minutes later. Ms. Afton drove away, Mort walked home holding our two clarinets, and the news vans headed back to their stations.

"Well?" I said, feeling nervous. "This has been, uh, quite a night."

"Yes. A little too much excitement, if you ask me," said the general. "Also very scary for the governor, when you two vanished into thin air." He gave both me and Emma a stern look. Then he turned to Kristen, who was standing on the bus steps, watching from a distance. "Excuse me," the general said. "I need to have a conversation with Kristen and find out how this happened."

"I'll be right there," said the governor. She turned back to me. "It's pretty late, so I think we're going to find a place nearby to stay the night. The rental SUV will take you home and then return to Detroit. We'll talk in the morning, okay?"

"Sure. Okay," I said. "Sounds good." There were a dozen other things I wanted to say, but this wasn't the right time.

Emma gave me a little wave over her shoulder, and she and the governor and the rest of the campaign team left on the Fresh Idea bus. Mom, Christopher, and I were left to ride home in the giant SUV that looked more like a tank than a truck.

I was about to climb into the SUV when Dad ran out of the company gate, waving his arms and shouting, "Aidan! Aidan, wait up!"

"Hey," I said, grinning. "What are you doing here?"

"I'm on break," he said. "I only have ten minutes, but I just wanted to say it's great to see you. And another thing. Nice job." Dad gave me a high five, then pulled me into an awkward hug.

"What part?" I asked.

"All of it," he said. "But especially when you tackled T.J. by the ankles."

"How did you see? Binoculars?" I asked, gazing up at the plant windows, which were tall and narrow—and slightly frosted-looking, as if they were meant to hide what went on inside, from spies and everyone else.

"No way. The security video," he said. "We were all watching." He smiled and wrapped his arm around my shoulders. "Glad you're back."

I smiled as if I really had hit a home run this time, instead of T.J.'s gut.

The next morning, I was back at home, watching TV with my brother. Everything was the same as it had been a week ago—except this time, Emma was sitting at the kitchen table with us. Plus, we no longer had cable.

Mom kept rushing around nervously, putting different snacks on the table in front of Emma. I could have told her not to bother, that Emma wouldn't eat anything she didn't know was peanut-free. *I* didn't have a special diet, though. I devoured five of Mom's special chocolate-chip pancakes in about a minute.

Emma sipped from a glass of lemonade and fanned herself with a section from the *Fairstone Free Record*, our town newspaper. It was all over the news that Senator Flynn's campaign had planted the story about my mom being a spy; as it turned out, there wasn't even a company *named* Cold Rainbow in China. Now he was the one defending himself on *Wake Up, America!*, saying he had nothing to do with the fake story.

Candace McKnight was grilling him and he was sputtering. *Thanks, Candace*, I thought, as if we were old friends, because we kind of were.

Also, just because the news station cameras hadn't captured my fight with T.J., that didn't mean it wasn't on TV. A couple of Christopher's friends had recorded it on cell phones and already posted them to YouTube, and the TV stations had captured those already. We were waiting to watch a brief press conference the governor was giving down at the town hall. She'd insisted it was okay if Emma and I stayed away this time. Personally, I think she was afraid I'd somehow knock her down again.

"Dude. Since when can you swing a bat like that?" Christopher asked me.

"It wasn't a bat; it was my clarinet," I said.

"Same thing. You nailed him." Christopher laughed.

"Maybe you should bat with your clarinet instead of a wooden bat from now on," said Emma. "You could be in the Little Musical League or something."

"Ha-ha," I said in a deadpan tone while Christopher cracked up.

"Good one," he said, still laughing. "Hey, at least this is a way better video to go viral than the one of you tackling the governor and getting frisked. In this one you actually look cool."

"You think so? Thanks," I said. His compliment meant a lot to me, more than I wanted to admit.

"Of course, that T.J. did nearly punch your lights out," Emma said, "until I came along."

"*You?* What did you do?" I asked. Was that typical or what? Emma trying to get all the credit when she hadn't even really been there until the end.

"He was about to flatten you. You would have been part of the parking lot if I hadn't come along," Emma said.

"You? It wasn't you; it was the general," I said.

But she and Christopher started laughing while my mom tried to hide the fact she was snickering, too, by biting her lip and turning to face the fridge.

"Okay, fine. Next time I won't try to save you from the class bully. See if I care," I said.

"Is there going to be a next time?" Emma asked. "I thought you were leaving the campaign. Isn't that why we came back here in the first place?"

"I guess I am," I said. I was glad to be home, but at the same time, I'd miss the excitement of being on the road and getting quoted right and left.

"You sure you don't want anything?" my mom asked, rearranging the plates of fruit, pancakes, and bacon in front of Emma.

"No, thanks," said Emma. "I'm going to wait for my mom and see if we can go out to a real restaurant for brunch."

Then again, some things about being on Governor Brandon's campaign I wouldn't miss, like Emma's snobby side.

She looked at me and coughed. "I mean, uh, actually that was something my mom said, that we'd go out later. I don't think I can wait that long, though. The fruit salad looks too good. I think I'll take some yogurt, too."

While my mom happily got her a bowl and spoon, my dad came home. After saying hi to Emma, he grabbed a plate and filled it with breakfast. He leaned against the counter beside Mom and watched the TV, because the governor had started her press conference, which she was holding outside the Fairstone town hall. She greeted the reporters and other guests, then looked right into the camera.

"This morning, I'm back in Fairstone, Ohio. I've been visiting with the people," Governor Brandon said. "I've been listening to what they have to say. I've also listened to my closest advisers. My husband. My children. My own intuition. But most of all, I've listened to you, the American public. Overwhelmingly, everyone's told me the same thing. I don't have to go far to find the best vice president for the job. He's right here in Fairstone with me."

I went weak in the knees.

"You?" Mom gasped.

"And so, without further ado, I'd like to announce my running mate for the November election." The governor smiled. "General Roy McGarvin, US Army, Retired." She turned to the general and held out her hand.

"What? Wait. You knew?" I asked Emma as I watched the general come to the mike and shake the governor's hand. They raised both hands together in a show of unity. Then, together, they started fielding questions from the press corps.

"They're totally going to win now, after what Flynn pulled," Dad said. "Don't you think? I can't believe I was going to vote for that guy."

Emma smiled. "Yeah. She just might."

Mom applauded. "What a smart choice. Oh, it's on," she said. "It's so on. After what Flynn did to us? Flynn's going down. Then we just have to focus on beating Mathias. I have to post this on Facebook right away!" She started tapping her phone's keys.

"Well?" I asked Emma. "Are you okay with this?"

"Definitely. As long as my mom listens to *me* next," she said, reaching for a glass of orange juice.

About an hour later, the governor, the general, and the Haircut stopped by the house for Emma. Kristen had been dismissed for losing track of Emma, which was too bad. It meant that another person would have to try to look after Emma and keep her safe from now on. Besides the Secret Service, that is.

"Wow. This is something I thought I'd never see," Dad said as he opened the door to let them inside, past the usual clutter of reporters on our lawn. "A retired army general like you, playing second fiddle to a woman? Can you handle that?" he asked.

"It's hardly second fiddle," the governor answered him. "I think of us as a team. Coworkers. The same way I'd want someone to consider me, if I were the vice president."

"Exactly." The general took a sip from the cup of coffee Mom had set in front of him. "I look at it this way. It's time for fresh ideas. If we don't try something new on the national level, how can we say we're a third party with fresh ideas?"

"Good point," Dad agreed, nodding.

"What next? Don't tell me, you're going to be secretary of state," I said to Stu.

"You never know." Stu picked up a strip of bacon and crunched it in his mouth.

"No, he's going to be secretary of haircuts. His first assignment will be you." The general smiled at me.

"This is a great breakfast, Tricia," Stu said. "Thank you very much."

"Yes, thanks. I have to admit I didn't eat much at the hotel," the governor said.

"Please, Governor Brandon, sit," my mom said to her, pulling back a chair at the kitchen table. "Fill up a plate and enjoy."

"Call me Bettina. And before I sit down, I have to tell you that we're extremely sorry," the governor said to my mom and dad. "Maybe it was naive of us, but we had no idea the campaign could get that ugly. We went back to meet with the CEO of FreezeStar, and he's assured us there are no problems with hiring you back, Tricia, once the economy picks up."

"Well, right, that's the key part," Mom said.

"But an interesting thing happened when we were sitting in his office. Some good news came in," the governor said, sliding onto the chair.

"Oh?" asked Dad. "Really?" He sat beside her.

"Orders are up. It's the publicity over the weekend. Everyone wants a union-made, U.S.-manufactured product," the general said.

"See, when you put pressure in just the right places, sometimes good things happen." The governor smiled, and so did my mom, who looked happier than she had in weeks. "This isn't a permanent solution to the issue. We know that. We'll keep working on it, and we'll keep listening."

"That's great," my mom said. "I know everyone here will really appreciate it."

"Well, so much of it is thanks to your son," said the governor. "In fact, I don't really know how to thank you, Aidan. You've given so much to us these past few days. You brought a spark to the campaign—"

"Yeah, and it almost went up in flames," I said.

She laughed. "Nothing my team can't handle. Right, General?"

"Definitely," said the general. "But at the same

time, if you can help us deliver the state of Ohio, we'll be even more grateful."

"About those Yankee tickets," I said. "It's not a big deal. I mean, I want to go, but I can wait. If you guys need the money for bumper stickers or whatever, that's okay."

"We'll get you the tickets," said the general, "but thanks. And if we win in November—"

"*When* we win," the governor interrupted.

"Right. *When* we win, we'll invite you to the inauguration, too. You and Emma can find more reasons to worry me to death," he said.

"Sounds good to me," said Emma, and we both laughed.

The governor turned to her daughter next. "And speaking of pressure, I know Aidan's leaving us here." She looked into Emma's eyes. "I have a pretty good feeling he's not the only one who wants to. You've had more than enough of the campaign trail, too, haven't you, Emma?"

Emma glanced from one side of the room to the other, avoiding her mother's gaze. "I have a confession to make," she said. "Mom, I might have done a few things to try to mess things up for you. I didn't want you to become president. But now, I do. So I'm sorry. But I do really want to go home. I mean, maybe I do still need to change my image, and I'll try really hard to use good manners and do everything right—I promise, Mom. But can I do it from home for a while? Maybe William could take my place."

"Can I be honest?" the governor asked. "It wasn't half as much about wanting to change you—that came from other people—as it was about missing you. The last year's been a killer, being away from home so much. I just wanted to hang out. But we hardly ever have time even to do that."

"Mom, we can find time to spend together. I'd just rather it's not on camera," said Emma. "So I'll stay out of the way, except for when you need me. Then I'll be there for you."

"That's good enough for me. And you don't have to change. For me, or anyone. Not even for *him*." The governor gestured over her shoulder at the general. "Just be yourself."

"I don't know. Aidan was himself, and look how well that went," said Emma.

"Shut up," I said.

"Let's go outside and play catch," she said. "They're only going to talk more politics."

We went outside into the front yard. Simon was leaning against my dad's truck, tossing a baseball into the air and catching it in his glove. "Thought you guys would never come out," he said.

"Tell me about it," I said. I grabbed my glove from the front steps, and tossed Emma's glove to her. "Let's play ball!"

AUTHOR'S NOTE

Would you like to spend your summer traveling with a presidential campaign and being a spokesperson for your town? Would you like to represent kids' issues in Washington, D.C.? How about running for vice president, or president?

You can probably do a lot of these things, but not until you're old enough to (a) leave home, (b) drive, and (c) vote. You'll have to finish high school first. And college. And get a job doing something that interests you.

Under the terms of the United States Constitution, anyone who wants to become the president must be a United States citizen and at least thirty-five years old. Also, a president must be a natural-born citizen, meaning that immigrants are not eligible to run for president, no matter how long they have lived in the United States. In addition, a presidential candidate must have actually lived in the United States for at least fourteen years.

So, it may be a ways off in your future, but in the meantime, you can still get involved. Look for volunteer opportunities in your community, or become a leader of your sports team, or help organize a school or family trip to the Capitol, or run for class president!

Check out **www.kids.gov and www.whitehouse. gov/about/white-house-101** to learn more about the U.S. government, and how it works. Interested in memorizing the names of U.S. presidents through history the way Aidan has? For an up-to-the-minute list of the presidents, visit: **www.whitehouse.gov/about/presidents**. The White House has an amazingly interesting site, packed with well-known and little-known facts. There's even an interactive tour of the White House! (In case Emma ever wants to really check it out.)

Lastly, I'd like to explain why I chose to write about a woman running for president—and one who is well on her way to winning the election. In the second presidential election I got to vote in, there was a woman on the ballot, Geraldine Ferraro. She was running for vice president, sharing the ticket with Walter "Fritz" Mondale, from Minnesota, for president. They lost to Ronald Reagan (#40) and George H. W. Bush, and for a long time it felt like the concept of a woman being on the ballot in November lost, too.

I kind of thought that every election cycle after that would include a woman on the ballot. Nope. It was another twenty-four years until Sarah Palin was chosen to run as vice president with John McCain. They also lost.

I didn't want to wait twenty-four years again, so I decided to make it happen. I also gave Governor Brandon the power to keep the Ford assembly plant in St. Paul, Minnesota, open, because I didn't want it to close. (As of this writing it is scheduled to close within the year.)

See, in my dreamworld, women get to be presidents, the same as men; kids can run for vice president, and no one who wants to work is ever out of a job.

What else should we dream about, while we're at it? A .400 batting average and a lifetime supply of Lime Brains candy?

Follow *your* dreams!

Catherine Clark has never been elected to office, unless you count being treasurer of the junior high student council. She has a long-term interest in politics, however, and majored in government in college. The author of numerous other books for young readers, she lives in Minnesota with her family. You can visit her online at www.hownottorunforpresident.com.